Moving Mama to Town

by Ronder Thomas Young

D0595522

A YEARLING BOOK

I gratefully acknowledge the support I received while writing this book from the Georgia Council for the Arts, the Society of Children's Book Writers and Illustrators, and Gina Maccoby.

Published by
Bantam Doubleday Dell Books for Young Readers
a division of
Bantam Doubleday Dell Publishing Group, Inc.
1540 Broadway
New York, New York 10036

Visit us on the Web! www.bdd.com

Educators and librarians, visit the BDD Teacher's Resource Center at
www.bdd.com/teachers

ISBN: 0-440-41455-5

Reprinted by arrangement with Orchard Books

Printed in the United States of America

November 1998

10 9 8 7 6 5 4 3 2 1

OPM

For William, Alec, and Ian

One

Big Kenny said that a real man doesn't stick around in the middle of a bad situation. A real man makes changes. Controls his own destiny.

Of course, the last time he said it, with his big hand resting on my shoulder, I didn't have any idea what it meant. I didn't see it coming, Daddy trading in all the corn for a truck and leaving us behind. Me, Mama, and Kenneth Lee. Once and for all. For good, I reckon. He's been gone since last summer.

Now that I've turned thirteen, I figure I'm man enough to take control of my own situation. My destiny.

We didn't put in much corn this year, not in any trading amounts, but I've got a few baskets of peas stashed. Not enough to trade for a whole truck, but surely enough for a good long ride out of here. Surely enough to get me to Elderton.

That was the old plan, to just get up and go, to leave Mama and little Kenneth Lee behind, same as my daddy, Big Kenny, did. I came up with it about the time Mama took up with that pasty-faced, mealymouthed, pea-

1

growing Custis Fullbright. About the time Kenneth Lee said, "I like Custis better than I ever liked Daddy. He's heaps nicer."

Kenneth Lee came right up to me and said that to my face. And I said right back to him, "Yeah. He's nicer because he don't give two cents what you do." I straightened up and put my hand on his arm. "He don't care what kind of man you grow into."

Kenneth Lee just shook off my hand. Stuck out his tongue and ran off. Sometimes I think he's not worth two cents. Most times I think he doesn't deserve to be running around with Daddy's name.

I thought about it a long time before I finally asked Big Kenny straight out. "Daddy," I said, "if you was set on having a junior take on your name, how come you didn't make it me? How come you made it Kenneth Lee?"

"Well, Freddy James," Big Kenny said, "everybody's got their strong points and their weak points."

Custis Fullbright gave short, stupid answers to questions. "Yes." "No." "So what?" Big Kenny, though, he gave wonderful long and confusing answers that made sudden, clear sense at the end.

"One of my points—I'm not sure yet whether to call it a strong one or a weak one—is not being too quick to trust other people." Big Kenny looked up. "Anybody," he said. "Nothing against your mother." He winked. "That's just the way I am."

"Yes sir."

"Well," he said, "after you'd grown a bit, more a boy than a baby, I could see plain as day where you came from." He smiled. Jabbed at his chest. "By the time little Kenneth Lee came along, I just took it on faith. Gave him my name."

"Oh." I didn't quite follow, but I could see Daddy was getting at something.

He shook his head. "I don't know what women are talking about, all the time going on about them little tiny babies, having the daddy's nose, the grandma's mouth." He looked close around my own nose and mouth. "You ever see any of that?"

"No sir," I said. And I wasn't lying.

Big Kenny nodded. "No harm," he said, "in taking your own sweet time in trusting anybody. You remember that."

"Yes sir."

He rubbed his hand through my hair. "What do you care, anyway, about being somebody's junior? You got your own good name. Be your own man." Big Kenny always made good sense in the end, but, truth is, I'm still waiting to understand the point of him up and leaving like that.

Custis Fullbright was a hired hand. Mama took him on after Daddy left to help bring in the corn, and by spring he was staying in the room over the barn. But even if he did sleep out there, he took every last one of his meals with us. And he had way more opinions than any hired hand ought to have. "I'm thinking, Miss John-

3

son"—Custis always called Mama "Miss Johnson," but he always winked when he said it, like it was a big joke— "I'm thinking you ought to give that whole east field up to peas." Stupidest thing I'd ever heard. Mama just went along with him. Worse than Kenneth Lee.

Each and every morning when I got up, I made a promise to myself that I wouldn't let Custis Fullbright get under my skin. Whenever I'd about had my fill of his foolishness, I'd just turn my attention to my plan about running off. It was a good one, and I was all set to put it into action, when Custis Fullbright up and beat me to it.

Mama might not know it, but I'd seen Custis Fullbright kiss her and move his chubby fingers up and down her bare arms. I reckon he was something a little more than a hired hand, and Mama is different since Custis left, but she's not the same kind of spooky crazy she was when Daddy didn't come home. I take some comfort in the clear fact that, even for Mama, losing Daddy and losing Custis Fullbright are two completely different situations.

It wasn't unusual for Daddy to take off by himself on a Saturday night, but it was unheard-of for him not to be there on Sunday morning pushing me and Kenneth Lee off to Sunday school, even though he never felt up to going to church himself.

"Still hope for you two," he'd say. "I'm a lost cause."

"You got that right," Mama would say, but she'd be there cooking up a stack of pancakes. She only did that on Sunday mornings. Over the years Daddy'd missed every kind of important event you can name at one time or another—it took a good long time to locate him when Kenneth Lee was born—but in all my years, I never knew Daddy to miss Sunday pancakes. I knew it that quick. Something was up.

But Mama, she kept up everything like normal for more than a week. Setting Daddy's place at the table. Letting on to Kenneth Lee that he'd just stayed out late and slipped out early. Threatening him with what Daddy would do if he came home and found he hadn't done any of his work out back.

'Round about Wednesday, supper time, Kenneth Lee figured it out himself. "He's gone, Mama," he said. "Daddy's not going to do nothing to me." We'd both heard some talk over at the school. Most everybody seemed to know Daddy was gone except for Mama.

Mama just laughed. "I'm warning you, boy," she said. "Get out there and do your chores before he gets back."

Kenneth Lee did them. Without any back talk. He went out the kitchen door and cut his eyes back at me through the screen. Daddy being gone was one thing. Mama gone plain crazy, that was another.

It took her about a week to get over it. Went through the whole craziness with the pancakes one more Sunday morning, but then I believe it was on Tuesday of that next week that she sat us down, before supper, and talked about what had happened. We'd already made a note of the fact that there were only three plates on the table.

We'd looked at each other, me and Kenneth Lee. Didn't say anything, but we both knew we'd moved on to something different.

Whenever it was time for Daddy to come in for supper—and for this last week, when she just pretended it was—Mama always took her hair down, brushed it out, and put it back up, smooth and in place. I always liked that. The way she'd take the time each and every ordinary day to fix up for supper. For Daddy. No matter how much they'd been bickering and carrying on in the morning. But that Tuesday night, when she only laid out the three plates for me and her and Kenneth Lee, her hair was slipping out all over her eyes and ears. She didn't look too good, but I felt better knowing she'd finally caught up with the situation. Daddy wasn't coming home.

"There's not anybody in the world," she said, not looking at us, even though she'd told us to sit down and listen, "that could spin a story like Big Kenny Johnson."

Kenneth Lee nodded. "I like the one about the cows, you know, when they got out and onto the main road, and—"

I kicked him under the table.

"Ow!"

Mama let out a long, long sigh. "I wasn't born around here," she said. "I was born on the coast, in South Carolina, in a little town called Saultee, not far from Charleston."

"Yes ma'am," Kenneth Lee said. "We know."

"Even my daddy liked Big Kenny." Mama smoothed out the hem of her dress. Pushed her loose hair back behind her ears. " 'I like the boy,' he said." She squinted. " 'But he's a gamble.' " She took in a long breath. Let it out. "That's what he said."

When Custis up and left, Mama got quieter. A little tighter around the mouth. Not as pretty somehow, all of a sudden, but not crazy.

"Always have a Plan B," Daddy said. "Expect the unexpected." So I haul some peas over to Hoyt Axel's in the old wagon. I plan a trade. The peas for the use of his pickup first thing Tuesday morning.

"How old are you, boy?"

"Sixteen." So okay, I might have to throw in a little extra just for him to overlook that lie and keep his mouth shut until I get back. I can't really spare the peas, but I don't want to come back and find Mama drowned in the creek, thinking I've run out on her, too.

It happens. Last time somebody drowned in the creek on purpose—and it was a woman—was when I was too little to remember it, but I've heard about it so much it's as good as a seen fact in my brain.

People, of course, drown in the creek with some regularity, especially in the spring, but an on-purpose drowning is different. Something to remember. And it would be just like my mama to be the one. And you think people would blame Big Kenny or Custis Fullbright for driving poor Eleanor Johnson to her death? No. They'd lay it right on the head of the last one to leave. That would be me. Her oldest son, Freddy James.

No man can live with that. A woman drowning herself in the creek on account of his leaving. Especially if the woman's that man's mother. So I'm not getting cheap with the peas. I let go of whatever it takes to keep Hoyt Axel's mouth shut.

"How long you think it'll take me to get into Elderton," I say.

"Oh." Hoyt squints up at the sun. "No more than an hour."

That leaves me three hours to figure the lay of the town, find myself a paying job, and find my mama a place to live.

"You got yourself a driver's license, boy?"

"No sir." Hoyt Axel enjoys giving me a hard time. Like I need a license just to drive into town and back. "You reckon I could borrow yours?"

That stops him. Hoyt scrunches up his nose. I figure he does that a lot—his nose has that red-and-white-stripe effect going across it. He shakes his head. "You'll be all right."

I pump his hand. "Well, thank you, sir." Look him hard in the eye. That truck better be there Tuesday morning.

"Okeydokey," Hoyt says. Gives a little nod. He knows it.

Soon as I turn around, I got to laugh. Like Hoyt Axel's got himself a driver's license.

TWO

I asked Custis once. Just once. I said, "Could I practice turning your truck around and backing down the cow path?"

"You finished out back?" he said. Like it was his concern.

"Yes sir," I said.

"No," Custis said. And he laughed. That's the kind of man Custis Fullbright was. Always laughing and winking. I reckon that's why Kenneth Lee took to him. I was old enough to know better.

I asked him just once. That's the kind of man I am. Kenneth Lee will carry on and whine until he gets whatever he wants. Not me. I don't ask twice. Didn't matter anyway. My daddy had shown me how to drive when I was a little kid.

"You can't reach anything," Daddy had said. "I just want you to get the idea, in case . . . in case you ever find yourself in a situation . . ." He cleared his throat. "Ever have to."

I nodded. Bobbed up and down between his legs.

Daddy pointed to the wheel. "Steering," he said. I nodded.

He pointed down. "Clutch. Gas. Brake."

One. Two. Three. "Yes sir."

He counted out the stick. "First. Second. Third." Shot his thumb backward. "Reverse." He looked at me. "You get it?" he said. "The principle of the thing."

"Yes sir." I squeezed the wheel. Bobbed up and down.

Except for the tractor, that was the last time I drove until today. I get right back into it. Easy. The way I've come 'round to think about it is that giving his boy the principle of things, that's the main thing a daddy's for. And maybe my daddy was just so good at it—at getting those principles across—he just finished up extra early with me.

Back before his green Chevrolet up and died, Daddy went into town every six weeks or so, and a lot of the times he took me with him. He never took Kenneth Lee. "Too rambunctious," he said. "I got business there." Daddy always got into town way quicker than an hour. He was a good, fast driver, a lot surer than me about the turns, and plus, that was back before Campbell Bridge was washed out, when you could go straight on across to 42.

Custis Fullbright never took me with him the times he went into Elderton, and I never asked him to let me go. If I had to be closed up in a vehicle with that sorry excuse for a man, I'd jump in the creek and drown on purpose myself.

So it's been awhile, but Elderton looks the same. Except for the hardware store, I never knew exactly where it was Daddy went. "I've got business to attend to" was all he'd say. He'd give me a dime. "Get yourself a cone." We'd meet up later at the bench outside the barber shop. I'd like to have gone in and gotten myself a proper town haircut, but Mama always kept us clipped pretty close. For all the times I've been in Elderton, I've never once been off this main strip. Barber shop, Henderson's Hardware, and Cooper's Drugstore. That's all I know.

I try Cooper's first. I can see myself doing that. Serving sodas. Filling up shelves. Something or other. Mr. Cooper's back at the drug section, pouring up pills. He looks up with that big old-man smile, just like he used to, when I came in to buy ice cream. But that was awhile back, and I don't see any need to try to get him to remember me. I just jump right into it.

"Mr. Cooper," I say, pulling up, tall and straight, like my daddy used to when he'd salute me. "My name is Freddy James Johnson, and I'm moving my mama and little brother into town, and I need a job." I clear my throat. "I'll do anything."

It comes back to me. Mr. Cooper was always too nice. He leans in and smiles. Looks kind of wet around the mouth. Makes me real uncomfortable. "On a holiday from school, are you?"

I hesitate. I don't want to get into this school thing, but I don't want to get caught up in an out-and-out lie either. "Less said, the better," Daddy always told me.

I remember in particular him saying it one time when the deputy sheriff came around asking questions about some business down the road.

"You mixed up in something?" Mama asked him.

Daddy shook his head. "Not as far as I know." He winked at me. "What I do know," he said, "is that nothing good ever comes of giving up reckless information."

Mr. Cooper himself, he's even got one of those old Uncle Sam posters, pointing right at me, letting me know that "Loose Lips Sink Ships." It comes back to me, the way Mr. Cooper was always asking questions. "In town for a visit?" he'd ask. "You got people here? We'd love to see you over at the church tonight for prayer meeting." He'd always hold on to the ice-cream cone until I mumbled something about my daddy and the hardware store. Couldn't just sell me a cone and be done with it.

"We're in town on some business," I say. I throw in the "we" just to be safe, but I reckon that does make it an out-and-out lie.

"My niece," he says, nodding toward the fountain in the corner, "now, she'll be working the fountain." A red-haired girl—about my age, I figure—dries and stacks soda glasses. "But you know, I could use a boy this summer for deliveries, maybe on Tuesdays and Thursdays?"

"That sounds good, sir," I say. "But I will have to run it by my mama first."

"Of course." He reaches for my shoulder.

I sidestep him. Smile. "Thank you, sir." I'd just as soon not let this fellow get a grip on me.

"I'll be looking for you, son."

I move real careful and slow. Until I get out the door. Then I run like the dickens. That was close.

I'd heard that in town they try to make you go to school, no matter how much work there is to be done. It wasn't that I didn't like school well enough, especially back when Miss Keitel still taught in Cole County.

One day Miss Keitel took one of those crime novels away from Mac Tower—his uncle in Atlanta sent them by mail every birthday and Christmas—and she had held it up, for all of us to see. "Now, this, I'll admit, is an adventure." Miss Keitel shook her curly blond hair. The girls snickered. "But," she said, holding up her own thin green book, "this is literature."

It was a long and fairly amazing story about this old war, the Trojan one, but mostly it was about this hellacious guy, Odysseus, trying to get back home to his wife. It was just one crazy situation after another, but still I could see what she meant about literature. There was a principle behind it.

And that is what I've been battling over ever since Custis Fullbright didn't come to supper that first night, ever since I'd seen I was going to have to go a different way.

Taking off, now that would be an adventure. But moving Mama to town, helping her pull herself up, helping Kenneth Lee maybe—just maybe—make something out of his sniveling self, now that would be literature.

So I'd learned that. I knew how to read anything that came my way. I always could figure faster than anyone around. So I was done with school as far as needing it. Then when Miss Keitel up and married that soldier and moved downstate, they brought in that slow-talking, skinny character with the round glasses and the bald head. Once he took over the school, all the fun went out of it, too.

I'm done with school. That was a mistake, going into Cooper's and getting caught up in his nosiness. I walk fast past Henderson's, the barber shop, and one of those ladies' stores. I have to do something. Walking fast isn't getting me anywhere.

Then I see it. Fenton's Fine Establishment. That's not up on just one sign, but three of them, all different colors—red, blue, and black. The red one is metal. It rattles when the screen door thwacks open and shut. And it thwacks a lot. People in and out. Laughing. Now that's a place of business.

Trouble is, I can't be certain exactly what that business is. An eating place, more than likely, but I think I ought to know before I go inside asking for a job.

A guy walks up. Takes off his hat. Scratches his head. Pulls open the screen door. Doesn't give me so much as a howdy do.

"Excuse me, mister." He comes back at me with a grin so loose and wide it can only mean one thing. Tipsy. "Excuse me, sir," I say. "Is this an eating place?"

"This is Fenton's, boy." His grin moves looser and wider. He waves his hat around. "Eat, drink, whatever you want."

I nod. "Thank you, sir."

He slams the door behind him.

An eating place. I can do that. Chopping up and frying and washing dishes. I can do that.

The screen door slams shut behind another fellow. Snaps me out of it. I've got to get Hoyt Axel's truck back soon. Might as well give it a try. I open up the door and walk inside.

There's a counter with stools all around it, and a few tables scattered here and there. Two men sit at the counter. Two men and a lady with red hair and a real loud laugh sit at a corner table. I never seen a lady with red hair in person before, and here this morning I've already seen two.

Behind the lady there's a long window. More light over there. A lot more people. A fellow holds up his stick and nods his head. I know what he's doing—studying those balls. I seen fellows take a good long look, then tell you exactly where those balls would end up. Side pocket. Corner. Art Crenshaw back home, he had a table in his barn, and Big Kenny used to take me over when he played. I always thought it was fairly amazing, when some fellow would up and tell you which balls were going where, and then it would happen just like he said.

The white-haired man at the counter turns around on his stool. "What can I do for you, son?"

There's a window to the kitchen behind the counter. Fellow pops his head through and stares at me. Smoke floats and curls over his head. I feel like it's reaching out, pulling around my neck, choking me. I cough.

The white-haired man raises an eyebrow. Looks like he might turn around on me. I know it. I feel it. This is a very important moment in my life, so I just blurt it right out. "I need a job, sir."

The fellow beside him turns around and takes a look. He has a thin little mustache.

"What kind of work is it you do?"

I take my time. I have to say the right thing.

The fellow with the mustache, he laughs.

"Steady work," I say. "I'll do anything."

The white-haired man squints. "What's your name, son?"

"Freddy James Johnson, sir."

The man with the mustache snickers. He puts me in mind of Custis Fullbright. That by itself makes me want to haul off and hit him. "Sometimes," Big Kenny had told me, "you got to screw your feet right tight into the ground and let God spell you." He was thinking at the time that maybe I shouldn't smack Mac Tower around, no matter what he might say, since his mama was such a good friend of my mama. Big Kenny balanced his hands, like a scale, up and down. "You got to weigh the consequences." So I screw my feet in, set my eyes straight on the white-haired man, and just ignore the other one.

He rubs his chin. "Miss Precious send you over here?"

I shake my head. "No sir."

"Your daddy?"

"Uh, no sir." I clear my throat. "My daddy's not coming. It's just me and my mama and my little brother."

"Well, Freddy James Johnson," he says, "they call me Fenton Calhoun, but if you're going to be working for me, I'll have to call you Fred." He snaps his fingers. "Things move a little quicker in town."

"That's fine, sir." I wonder if he can hear my heart thumping.

The fellow with the mustache snickers again. "Come on now, Fenton, ask him what he won't do. Nobody does *everything*. Ask him what he won't do."

I screw my feet in tighter. The red-headed woman in the corner lets loose again. Loud and unladylike. I look down into the dark end of this room and wonder what it opens into.

"Well?" Mr. Calhoun grins, too, but I overlook it. I have a good feeling about him.

"Well, I'd rather not do anything to break the law, Mr. Calhoun, seeing as how I have to look after my mama and all."

Mr. Calhoun nods. "Fair enough." Stands up. Holds out his hand. "When can you start?"

"Day after tomorrow. I got to move Mama in and—"
I bite my tongue. Daddy was always saying not to do
that. "If that's okay."

"Fine and dandy," Mr. Calhoun says. "And where
you going to be moving your mama to?"

"Well," I say, "I got to work on that next."

The man with the mustache laughs.

"I got a place in the back," Mr. Calhoun says, "but
I don't rightly see anybody's mama living there." He
sits back down on his stool. "You better go work out
something with Miss Precious."

I just stand there.

"He don't know Miss Precious?" The mustache man's
eyes bulge. Sounds as if that ends it all. As if hiring
Freddy James Johnson is the biggest, craziest thing he
thinks Mr. Fenton Calhoun could ever do.

Doesn't faze Mr. Calhoun though. He hunkers down
on his stool and points through the screen. "See that big
yellow house? Up on the hill?"

I unscrew my feet and hunker down with him. Nod.
Hard to miss.

"That's where you'll find Miss Precious Doolittle.
She'll fix you up."

"Yes sir," I say. "Thank you, sir." I back to the screen
door. "I'll be here, day after tomorrow, sir."

Mustache man laughs. Someone yells out a string of
curse words from the pool room.

I push open the screen.

"Fred," Mr. Calhoun says. "Hold up."

I turn around.

"Your mama didn't send you over here then?"

"No sir."

Mr. Fenton shrugs. "Well, just so you don't get some outsize notion of your own charm, the minute I laid eyes on you, I could see you were Big Kenny's boy."

Mustache man's mouth falls open. "Big Kenny Johnson?"

Mr. Calhoun nods.

"Yes sir." I walk regular as long as I think they might see me, then set out running for that big yellow house.

Three

It's farther than it looks. Past row after row of houses. I set into running. A little kid pulling a wagon barrels past me. He's hauling another kid who howls like a fire engine.

A man's voice calls out. "Somebody after you, son?" I whip my head around. Can't see exactly where it comes from.

The fellow at the gas station holds out his nozzle, hangs open his mouth, and stares me down, but he doesn't say anything.

I know how it must look. Stranger running like a demon through the middle of town. Like somebody's after him. Like he's up to no good.

I couldn't stop even if I wanted to. It's like I'm flying to that yellow house up on the hill, up over the whole town, getting bigger and bigger. My heart has gone plumb wild, like some crazy animal trying to beat itself out of my chest. I'm not tired. I'm strong and fast and I could run up and down the whole day long without giving out. It's not like my heart's beating so fast because

I'm running so fast, but more like my body's got to move to keep up with my heart.

I never felt anything like this.

I did it. I got a job.

The big green hill just sort of bumps into me, and I look up at the yellow house. I try to slow down my breathing, but it's like my heart won't stop hammering. I think I might vomit. And I know I can't.

A lady like Miss Precious Doolittle, who lives in a big house like this, might not have anything to do with the likes of me. I'm fairly plain myself, but I can't even say for a fact that I'd do business with some stranger that just ran up into my yard and vomited.

I take a deep breath. Get over it. Take another one. Start up the hill.

"Boy?"

I'd got past all those others, staring me down, wondering what my business was, and I'm not about to be stopped by anybody's nosiness now. I slow down, but I don't stop.

"Over here, boy." It's an old man with a rake.

I stop. "Sir?"

"Over here." A woman's voice.

I turn. The woman comes out from a stand of trees behind the man, and at the same time, he sort of disappears into them. She seems a lot bigger than the man, but I reckon she's not really. It's her voice. It carries. Makes her seem big. She's kind of old herself. White hair pulled up in a bun. Wrinkly around the cheeks. All the same, she makes you want to take a couple of steps back. She's got a big, strong air about her.

"Yes ma'am." I reckon you can't just run right up to a house like that. Reckon it's not safe to make it easy. Everybody and anybody would be there wanting to take a look.

"Your name Fred?"

I blink. I remember it is. "Yes ma'am."

Motions to the trees. "Come on then." I'm supposing this must be Miss Precious Doolittle, but it doesn't seem right, a rich lady wearing overalls and those ugly brown shoes. "Fenton gave me a call about you." She comes to an upside down half-barrel and sits down.

There's another barrel, over a ways, under another tree, but it seems like I'm supposed to stay put. "Yes ma'am."

She takes her first good look at me, as far as I can tell. "What makes you decide to move into town right now?"

"I been planning it for a while, ma'am."

"Fenton's got that little room in the back, you know. That'd cost you next to nothing." She swats a fly away from her nose. "Jacob's leaving in a couple of days. Didn't Fenton tell you that?"

I figure it's best to act like I know what's going on. Like I know who Jacob is. Like I know for sure who she is. "Yes ma'am," I say, "but you see I've got my mama and my brother to worry about."

Her face changes. Wrinkles up even more. Her eyebrows move together into one long one. "Your mama send you into town?"

I shake my head. "No ma'am."

She straightens up. Rubs her chin. That might have been the wrong thing to say. "Brother?" she says. "How old is this brother?" She's got a suspicious air about her.

I search my brain for what might be the right answer. What would it matter to her how old Kenneth Lee is? I don't know, so I settle on the truth. "Nine."

She looks down. Wipes her hands together, like she's trying to get something off, like she's just come up from working in the dirt. Shakes her head. "That's a rowdy age. Nine years old."

I see now where it's going. She doesn't want a little kid messing up her place. "Yes ma'am," I say. "That's the usual case." Pull my lips as straight and my face as long as I can. "But little Kenneth Lee—that's my brother—he's been sickly almost from the time he was born."

She makes a noise. It's a low noise, sort of a snort, and to herself. I think she might be laughing at me, but it's hard to tell.

"You think, ma'am, you might have a place for us?" I know now this has to be Miss Doolittle, but all the same, I'm afraid to call her by name outright. And we're too far along for me to just plain ask her.

She looks up. Smiles for the first time. Two gold teeth, one on each side of her mouth, sparkle. "So you're Big Kenny's boy?"

I nod. At first it made me nervous, the way everybody knows Daddy. Especially since I don't have any idea where he is. Or why. It's like these people might know more about him than I do. But now I'm getting comfortable with the idea; it's almost as if I'm not by myself. Like having people know I'm Big Kenny's boy is almost as good as having him right alongside me.

"I've done some business over the years with your daddy." She squints at me. "I reckon he must have mentioned that to you, though."

"No ma'am."

She nods. She snorts that little laugh again. Then goes suddenly serious. Pulls a folded piece of paper out of her top pocket. "I got two places. One upstairs on River Street for twenty a month. Another on Beacon, with your own bath, for twenty-seven a month."

"I'll take that first one. The twenty."

"You might want to take a look at it, son."

Shake my head. "I don't have time today, ma'am. I've got to get back to the farm."

She studies me for a minute, then nods. "Okay then." She presses the paper against her knee and writes on it with a pencil she pulls out of that same pocket. Tears off a strip and holds it out to me. "Now, I want you to be clear on this. Normally, there's up-front money. Security deposit and a month in advance. We'll let that go this time. But if you take this paper without looking at the place, I don't want you showing up here with

24

your mama and changing your mind. I don't have time for foolishness."

I take the strip of paper. "No ma'am." I fold the paper and stick it deep in my pocket. I take her hand and pump it—"At least three times," Big Kenny always said. "Thank you, ma'am." I try not to mumble.

She takes a key out of her side pocket and gives it to me. "There's two beds furnished," she says. "A sofa. And a dinette."

"Yes ma'am." I hadn't counted on any furniture at all. That'll make things way easier.

She looks at me. "You heard from Big Kenny lately?"

I shake my head. "No ma'am."

"So he didn't tell you to come see me?"

"No ma'am. It was that Mr. Calhoun."

She shrugs. "All right." Waves me away. "You can go now."

"Thank you, ma'am." And I run, following my beating heart back to Hoyt Axel's truck. Faster and faster. I wave to the gas station attendant this time around. Elderton's my town, too.

Four

I'm not scared of a fight. Especially not one I'm bound to win. On the drive back to Hoyt Axel's I go over and over it in my head. On the run back home I work it out perfect.

"We're just supposed to up and move into town?" That's what I figure Mama'll say. "On your say-so?"

"What else we going to do?" I'll answer right back. "Work this farm forever?" Judging by her face, if I don't think it'll hit her too bad, I'll add, "Daddy's gone, and it don't look like he's coming back."

What does scare me, once I'm back home, face to face, and laying it all out for Mama, is how quiet she takes it. Her head nods. Her eyes brighten up. She doesn't interrupt once. Mama's usually real quick to disagree.

Kenneth Lee jumps in complaining, though. "What you talking about? Where you been all day?"

"What are we going to do? Work this farm forever?" I go ahead and use my answer for Mama on him. She doesn't seem to need it.

Kenneth Lee stares at me. "What?"

I guess it doesn't make good sense. Not without the right question. But I try to keep him on track. "Daddy's not coming back to help us, you know."

"Well, if you'd do your part," he says, "instead of running off all day."

Kenneth Lee's a waste of time.

"No," Mama says. "I think Freddy James has got himself a real good idea here." She smiles and looks out the window. "I could get a job, maybe cleaning up some well-to-do lady's house or . . ." She looks back at me. "Maybe even in that dress shop . . . where your daddy bought me that hat." She smooths back her hair. Nods toward her bedroom. "You know. The pink one. For Easter Sunday?"

Kenneth Lee's mouth falls open. You can see he wants to jump in, like he always does, but he just can't get a handle on this particular conversation. Truth is, I started it, and I'm having trouble keeping up myself. "I got a job," I say.

Mama raises her eyebrows.

Kenny sees his chance. He snorts. "In the dress shop?"

I'm thinking, he likes this place so much, maybe he can just stay on behind, while me and Mama move to town. "No," I say. "Working for Mr. Fenton Calhoun, in a sort of eating place, I guess."

"More of a saloon, from what I've heard." Mama's eyes narrow. Maybe I'll have a fight after all.

"I saw people eating," I say.

Mama folds her hands together, almost like she's praying, but instead of closing her eyes, she fixes them right straight ahead on me. "Okay then," she says.

That's what she says, but I'm feeling like she's not getting it, not even as good as Kenneth Lee. "Mama, my job starts day after tomorrow. We got to pack up and go in the morning."

"Pack up and go where?"

"I got us an apartment."

Mama's mouth falls open.

"There's this lady, this Miss Precious Doolittle—"

Mama nods her head. "Miss Precious." She opens up the oven and takes out a pan of cornbread.

"A what?" Kenneth Lee says. "A part of what?"

"You know Miss Precious?" I ask.

"A part of what!" Kenneth Lee yells.

Me and Mama, we both look at him. Mama squints, then laughs. "A part of a whole house. An *apartment.*"

Kenneth Lee puzzles up for a second, then just shrugs. Lets it go.

Mama looks at me. "We've met," she says. "Me and Miss Precious." She nods at the stove. "Supper's ready." Kenneth Lee picks up the bowl of beans. I take the greens. Mama sets down the rice and cornbread. The usual supper. Just as good as always.

"No tomatoes?" Kenneth Lee asks.

Mama nods over toward the windowsill. "Slice one up if you want." She taps her fingers on the edge of the table. Slowly. Like counting off something in her head.

Kenneth Lee shrugs. Takes another piece of cornbread instead.

"You think this Miss Precious is okay then?" Miss Precious knows Daddy. Mama knows Miss Precious. I don't know what's what anymore.

"I think she's as good as her word." Mama wipes her mouth. "You give her any money?"

I shake my head. "Not yet." Now where's she think I'd get money? I reach down into my pocket and come out with the key. "I've got a key though."

Mama nods. "All right." She taps her fingers on the table. "Seems like Minnie said something to me about Johnny taking them into town tomorrow." Squints her eyes. "Something about Mac needing new shoes." Stands up. "Maybe we can get a ride." Points at Kenneth Lee. "You wash up these dishes." And to me, "Start packing."

She's out the door. Gone. Instead of walking or even running, she hops on my old bicycle leaning against the coop. Kenny and me watch her through the window. We've never seen Mama on a bicycle. I cannot believe it. Kenny is, thankfully, struck dumb.

I know Mama's got a suitcase. A few times when she got really mad at Daddy she set it out on her bed, but Daddy would always just laugh and put his arm around her. "Where do you think you're going?" he'd say, and kiss the top of her head.

I never worried about Mama leaving. She'd always

29

end up laughing herself and put the suitcase back up in the closet. It's not there now though. I pull some burlap bags out of the pantry and give one to Kenneth Lee. "Clear out your drawers," I say, "and put your clothes in here."

"All of them?"

"Yeah."

"We really going?"

"Yeah."

"What if Custis comes back?"

I glare at him.

"Or Daddy? Or anybody?"

"We're not going all that far away." In actual fact, I feel like I'm flying right out of this world, but I don't think I better tell Kenneth Lee. One thing I do know, after seeing the way Mama took the news, I could tell her. And I think she'd say, "Me, too, Freddy James. Me, too." I'm not a bit scared anymore.

Kenneth Lee goes back to his drawers and stuffs his clothes in the bag. I stand in the kitchen, running down in my mind what we all use in the course of a regular day. Well, for sure, we'll need plates and cups and knives and spoons and forks. I count out three each and set them in the dishpan. Mama's carving knife and her big pot and her iron skillet. That ought to do it for eating. Look around the sitting room. Move the lamp and the afghan over beside the dishpan. Feel in my pocket for the key. Pull out the piece of paper. 17-B River Street.

Kenneth Lee drags his half-filled bag out. "Can I take my deck of cards?"

I can't see as I was ever that stupid. "Yeah. We're leaving. Take everything you want that'll fit in that bag."

"What about Josie?"

His chicken. I reckon of all of us, Kenneth's the most connected to this farming life. "No," I say. "Not Josie." I don't know why I add it on, but I say, "Not right yet."

I don't mean anything by it, but Kenneth Lee smiles like I do. Goes back and rakes his cards, some little book, and those tin trucks Daddy bought for him into his bag.

Mama rushes—face red, hair flying—through the door. "Johnny said if we're ready to go by seven, they'll be happy to take us." I wonder how happy Johnny really is, but then Minnie Tower's pretty much my mama's best friend.

"Nothing but a troublemaker," that's what Big Kenny used to say about Minnie Tower. "With her silly talk and her movie magazines." The same uncle that sends Mac those crime novels sends Minnie magazines about movie stars and beauty and such, and when she's done with them, she passes them on to Mama.

Mama looks at Kenneth Lee, standing in the door, holding onto his lumpy bag. She kneels down and looks into it. "Good job," she says. Kisses him. "Go on to bed now. We're going to have a lot of excitement tomorrow."

"Don't I have to go to school?" Kenneth Lee asks.

Mama shakes her head. "You've only got the week left before school's out." Nods at me. "We'll get you both back on track next year."

I had tried to go back to school after Christmas, but that old man didn't have anything new to say, far as I could hear. Plus, I just squirmed and sweated the whole time, worrying about what Custis Fullbright was up to. Two days was about all I could take of that.

"I need to be home to keep an eye on that fellow." I told Mama that right to her face. I expected her to fight me on it, but she didn't.

Kenneth Lee hugs Mama. Goes on off to bed without a word. I think he's too confused to do anything else.

"I got some kitchen stuff together," I say.

Mama looks over at the dishpan and nods. "Good." She pulls out two more of everything. "For company," she says.

Company. That's what she called Custis Fullbright at first. I can do without company.

She pulls down a shoe box from the top pantry shelf, sits down at the kitchen table, and shuffles through the papers in it. Fast the first time, then slowly, one by one.

"What's all that?" I say.

Mama shakes her head. "Important papers. Birth certificates and whatnot." She looks up at me. "Get another one of those bags and fill it with bedclothes and towels."

"Where's your suitcase?"

I drag a chair back and check that closet shelf one

more time. Reach all the way to the back. Get down and go back to the kitchen. "Maybe it got moved out to the shed."

Mama shakes her head. "I said your daddy took it, Freddy James." She sighs and puts the lid back on the box.

I don't know what to make of Daddy running off with Mama's suitcase. It was Mama's from before they were even married. It had her old initials—ERS, for Eleanor Ruth Sullivan—in gold letters on the top. I guess he had a reason, but I don't see how it could be a good one.

Five

Mama shakes us out of bed before daylight. "Get on out to the field," she says. "You ought to be able to get a fair amount of greens, maybe some peas and carrots."

Except for the greens, we don't come back with much. "It's too early," I say.

Mama nods. She fills up one basket just for us. "Leave the rest on the kitchen table," she says.

We try to pack light. Put back two things for every three we almost take with us, thinking we can probably live without it, at least for a little while. Still, even going with just the bare bones, it adds up. We stand out front in a circle of burlap bags and bushel baskets full of stuff. "Like a band of gypsies," Mama says. She holds her hands over her mouth and taps her fingers together. She draws circles in the dirt with her feet. Kenneth Lee feeds the chickens. I'm about to jump out of my skin.

Johnny Tower pulls up in front of the house and climbs out of his truck. Folds his arms and sighs. "You sure about this, Eleanor?"

"Yes, I am," Mama says. She picks up a bag.

Johnny lets down his tailgate. Nods at me. "You?"

"Yes sir." I pick up the biggest bag and slide it into the truck.

Minnie grabs Mama and gives her a big hug. "If that woman knew something," Daddy always said, "she'd be dangerous." But the way he looked at her, when he'd come upon Mama and Minnie Tower going over Minnie's new stack of magazines from Atlanta, you could tell he thought she was dangerous enough as it was.

"How's she get her hair to do that?" Daddy would flip his hands around his head.

"Sugar water," Mama said. "And snuff cans."

"Say what?" Daddy said.

Mama would demonstrate, rolling her hair around her fingers. "The sugar dries up stiff and keeps the curl nice."

"Well, just don't you try it," Daddy said.

Kenneth Lee and Mac help me finish loading up the back. Minnie takes Mama's hands. "I just can't believe it." She looks up at the sky and shakes her curly blond hair. "You're moving back to South Carolina."

Mama laughs. "I hadn't thought about it that way." She looks at Johnny. "We collected what we could. Good many greens." Tilts her head toward the screen door. "In the kitchen."

Johnny nods. "I'll probably be going down end of the week." He's helped us out a lot, taking whatever we had with him when he went to the farmers' market. Me

35

and Kenneth Lee and Mac shove the bags and baskets around and find ourselves a spot. "All aboard," Johnny says. He closes the tailgate and climbs in behind the wheel. Minnie pushes Mama in beside Johnny and climbs in after her.

South Carolina. I hadn't given any thought to that. We're not just moving into town. We're moving into a completely different state. Sure, I know you pass the state line on the way into Elderton, but the fact never meant much to me before. Today, though, I'm wishing that old sign they used to have, the one that said "Leaving Georgia," hadn't rotted away. Leaving the state. That's something. It is.

Minnie Tower's talking up a storm. Hands moving. Head bouncing. Makes Mama look small, with all that motion. Minnie Tower's hair is as Hollywood blond as I ever hope to see in real life.

"I see old Minnie's been hitting the bottle again," Daddy would say. He'd wink at us and add, "The peroxide bottle."

Mama might laugh a little at Daddy's Minnie jokes, but she never said anything against her, and there wasn't any doubt she liked visiting with Minnie. She'd laugh more. Talk faster. For hours after Minnie had gone home. Today, though, when Johnny stops and Mama climbs out, she's pale and doesn't have much to say. Might just be the combination of Johnny and Minnie. Once Minnie reached over and grabbed at his hand on the wheel, and he turned around and yelled at her.

Couldn't hear what he said, over the wind, but I could sure see it was loud.

Of course, Mama could just be feeling sick from the bumpy ride. Johnny could use some new shocks. He said so himself.

"Why don't you boys settle in here, and Eleanor and me, we'll go over to the dress shop, see if she might get herself a job." Minnie's hands are all over the place.

Mama shakes her head. "I don't think so." She looks up at the two-story house in front of us. It's brown. Not a natural wood brown. Flat, mud brown. She looks at me. "Is this the place?"

I check the paper again. "Seventeen-B." Look at the number over the door. "This is River Street? Right?"

"One and only," Johnny says. Points to the house next door. "Nineteen," he says. Points to a couple across the street. "Sixteen and Eighteen," he says. Nods at the brown house. "This is it." He puts his arm around my shoulder and pulls me aside.

"Mac," Minnie says. "Help Kenneth Lee with those bags."

"Don't worry about the critters or . . . I'll help your mother take care of that end, and you just do your part on this one."

"I sure do appreciate it, Mr. Tower."

"No trouble, son." He laughs, but not in a funny way. "I reckon I'd have had to do a lot more if . . . if you'd run off like your daddy." He grasps my shoulders with his two hands. "That's a good piece of land, son," he says. "You could make a go of it, if you tried."

"Yes sir," I say, "but I think this is for the best."

Johnny straightens up. "I reckon so." Sighs. I know what he's thinking. He's thinking that if he lives to be a hundred he'll never up and leave his land to move into town, and he'll never understand anyone who would.

I shake his hand. Three times. Up and down. He won't let Minnie come inside. "We got to get the boy some shoes. Go by the bank. I got to get back." He looks at Mama. "We'd be happy to come back and visit proper, Eleanor, when you and the boys are all settled."

Johnny drives away. Mac sticks out his tongue. Minnie hangs out the window waving. Mama waves, too, but she lets out a long sigh when they turn the corner. "Sometimes it's hard to keep up with all of Minnie's ideas." She picks up one of the bags. "You say you got a key?"

I run up to the door and stick the key in the lock, but the knob turns on its own. A tall, pale, blond lady opens the door wide. "Hello," she says. "You must be the Johnsons." She holds out her hand. I wonder if Mama's going to take over now, but she doesn't step up. Doesn't say anything.

I take the lady's hand. "Yes ma'am." Pump it.

"I'm Susannah Doolittle," she says.

"Doolittle?" Mama raises her eyebrows.

Susannah Doolittle's face tightens. "Miss Precious's daughter," she says. "Her adopted daughter."

Mama smiles and nods. "Oh."

The hallway's dark. To the left there's what looks like a rug hanging on the wall. It's real nice though. There's a scene on it. I make out dogs and horses and trees. I reckon if I had a rug that nice, I'd hang it on the wall, too, to keep it clean. I catch Kenneth Lee's eye. Nod at the rug. His eyes widen. He leans in to study it. I've sort of got a headache. I'd like him to stay happy for a while. Keep down the complaining.

"This," Miss Doolittle says, "is the door to my apartment." She puts her hand on the knob, but she doesn't open the door. "I give French lessons in my parlor, and when I have students over, I must ask that you keep a low level of noise." She looks directly at Kenneth Lee. "I'm sure you understand."

Kenneth Lee's mouth falls open.

"French lessons." Mama lowers her head. Like she's praying. After a moment she looks back up at Miss Doolittle. "You speak French."

"Not particularly well." Miss Doolittle starts up a side staircase. "But well enough, I'd say, for all the use it gets in Elderton."

I follow her. Miss Doolittle isn't exactly what you call pretty. She's pale. Her face is long and horsey. But her voice makes regular words sound like singing. Don't know that I've ever actually heard French talking, but the thought of her doing it sort of takes my breath away.

"This is a special house," she says, "in a strange and sad way." She laughs. "It was the first one Miss Precious had fixed up, and it didn't turn out quite right."

The stairs end up right smack into a wall. Mama looks at Miss Doolittle.

"Just to your left, then right back around." She shakes her head. "Don't ask me how that happened."

We all weave around the narrow landing into a sunny room. Miss Doolittle nods. "This is it." It's just a sofa and a rug and a lamp. I'm right pleased to see the lamp. Through an open door I see a bed. I'm hoping there's another one. "Now, Miss Precious doesn't supply any shades or curtains on upstairs windows." She waves her hands. "Plenty of tree cover."

Mama nods.

"Come winter, though, you might want to think about doing up something yourself."

Kenneth Lee tries to push up a window. Mama peeks through the next door.

"That's our kitchen." Miss Doolittle pushes past Mama and waves us in. Me and Mama and Kenneth Lee huddle together in the doorway. Miss Doolittle points to the left. "Those are my cupboards." She points to the right. "Those are yours." The doors are all open and empty. "The rest—" She waves her hand across the stove, refrigerator, and big double sink. "The rest I think we'll just work out in a decent and civil manner."

Our kitchen? I look back at Mama. That idea doesn't seem to bother her.

"Of course," Mama says.

"I'm not much for cooking anyway." Miss Doolittle

points to a door over in the corner. "That's to the stairs that run down to my apartment. I share the bath as well, right through here." Mama pokes her head in. Nods. "Then this . . ." Miss Doolittle shakes her head. "This is just extra space. You can use it."

I look in. There's a window. I like it. "I call this," I say.

Mama nods. Miss Doolittle folds her arms. "You see, in most of Miss Precious's houses, you get two families sharing upstairs, kitchen and bath in the middle, with the one big apartment downstairs. But that Bill Campbell, he made a royal mess of this place. Miss Precious was furious. He had to move down to Savannah to get any work after that." She shrugs. "The layout doesn't make sense, and it's not particularly attractive, but then you get more space out of it." She waves toward the extra room and smiles at me.

"It's lovely," Mama says.

I think she means it.

"So anyway, I'm glad to have you."

"I'm Eleanor." Mama holds out her hand. "I don't reckon I told you that."

Susannah takes it. "Like Mrs. Roosevelt?" She looks delighted.

Mama sighs. "Yes." Mama says Mrs. Roosevelt is a smart lady, but I think she's getting tired of having the same name.

Miss Doolittle unfolds her arms. "Any questions?"

I'm wondering why Miss Precious Doolittle's adopted daughter lives in this messed-up brown house instead of the big yellow one, but it's Mama who says, "I was just wondering. Who takes the French lessons mostly, grown-ups or children or—"

"Women, mostly. Young and old." Miss Doolittle smiles. "They got interested during the war. Wanted all those men coming back from overseas to hear a few foreign words at home, so they'd realize there was nothing really too special about those French girls." She shrugs. "They just kept coming after that, for whatever reason."

Mama nods. She doesn't smile.

"Oh yes," Miss Doolittle says. "There's a telephone down in the front hall if you need it." We never had a telephone before. The Towers did. That's the number we gave out for emergencies, at school and the like.

Miss Doolittle puts her hand on the knob of that corner door, then turns back and looks right at me. "Miss Precious took quite a liking to you, Fred. I'm surprised she didn't adopt you, too."

Mama's head jerks up. "He's got a mother."

Miss Doolittle looks at Mama. Her eyes are sharp, but her voice keeps that same softness. "Of course he does," she says. "I only meant that she took a liking to him." She looks back at me. "She said that you looked to her to be a young man with a lot of gumption." She gives Mama a thin, little smile. "Miss Precious likes gumption." She opens the door. "Well, good day." Closes the door.

Me, Mama, and Kenneth Lee, we stand there and listen to her footsteps tap down the stairs. A second door opens and closes. I look back around *our* kitchen. This town life will take a little getting used to.

Six

If I eat more than two pieces of Mama's double-chocolate devil cake, I sort of go crazy. Tapping my feet. Talking fast. Then all of a sudden just settling into being dog-tired and sick. Mama says it's the sugar that has that up-and-down effect.

That's what it's like now, sitting around in this strange room, with all these baskets and bags scattered around. We don't really feel at home with any of the furniture yet, so we just spread out on the floor.

Getting a job, getting here, taking on all this change, all in two days, is like digging into that third piece. This is the dog-tired and sick part.

Mama hands me a piece of cold cornbread from last night. "I'm sorry," she says. "I should have thought to put on some beans when we first came in."

"That's all right," I say. I'm too tired to care about beans. It sure would be nice to have a piece of cake right now, though. When it's cool, Mama smooths pure fudge all over what's already gooey and black and sweet and good enough to eat plain.

"It's a sin and a luxury," Mama says. Double-chocolate devil cake only comes once a year. At Christmas. And during the war we had to skip one of those.

With Daddy and Kenneth Lee and neighbors dropping by, you never knew how long it would last. And the way stuff kept happening, like the war and the drought and the flash floods, you never knew for sure if you'd ever see another one. I always went for that third piece. Like Daddy said, "Got to get while the getting's good."

"What time is it," Mama asks, "that you got to be at this job?"

I don't trust her tone. Like no matter what I say, it won't be the right answer. "Early as I can, I guess."

"Hmmph." I knew it. Getting here, it's a fine idea. Now that we're smack in the middle of it, she's going to find something wrong. "And what's he going to be paying you?"

"Enough." I don't know. Why didn't she ask me that last night if it's so important?

Kenneth Lee lays his head down on Mama's lap. "Keep your eye on that Fenton Calhoun," she says.

I nod. She's probably right about that. I bet Daddy would tell me the same thing. "Mama," I say. "When you met Miss Precious, was it at her house?"

Mama nods. She rubs Kenneth Lee's hair back. He closes his eyes.

"The big yellow one?" I ask. "Did you go inside?"

"Sure I did," she says. "So did you."

I shake my head. "No, we talked outside. She didn't invite me in."

"Well," Mama says, "I don't recollect that she *invited* me in." She laughs. "All I know is I *went* in." Points at me. "And so did you. Perched up on my hip, with that little bald head of yours bobbing around, taking it all in."

We both wait for Kenneth Lee to start giggling, like he always does when Mama talks about me being a bald-headed baby. He must be asleep. "What were we doing there?" I'd never have had the nerve to just march in on Miss Precious without her telling me to.

Mama sighs. "It was that time your daddy went off to the State Farmers' Market, and . . . forgot his way home." Kenneth Lee curls his legs up. Mama reaches over to the pile of blankets and pulls one up over his feet. "I was mad as the dickens." Mama eases her right leg out from under Kenneth Lee. Stretches it out. Makes a face. "Cramp," she says.

"Forgot his way home?"

"I went over to Minnie's"—Mama shakes her head—"and just spent the afternoon crying my eyes out." She flexes her toes up. "Then Johnny comes in and says if I'd just dry up and go home, he'd take me into Elderton in the morning to talk to Miss Precious."

"How come?"

Mama nods. "That's what I wanted to know. I'd never heard of the woman." She eases Kenneth Lee's head off her leg and onto another blanket. Rubs her leg. "Gone to sleep," she says. "Johnny didn't know either. seems that's what people do in these parts. Go see Miss Precious. See what she'll do. What she has to say."

"What'd she do?"

"She let me in her house and listened to me carry on about how I'd had enough of that farm, and that I was leaving, and how I'd appreciate it if she'd get a message to that effect to Big Kenny, if she could."

"Where were you going?"

"Back home. To Saultee."

"Well—" I sit up straight. I wonder if she for once actually packed up that suitcase with her initials on it. "Were you taking me with you?"

She laughs. "Now, what else was I going to do with a little bald-headed baby?" Shakes her head. "Of course, I wouldn't have really gone back home. I wasn't ready to listen to my daddy go on with his 'I told you so.' " She looks at me. "Your Grandpa Sullivan liked your daddy, he just didn't think he was one to settle down."

"Did Miss Precious help you?"

Mama shrugs. "Hard to tell. She gave me a look like I was trash off the street, but she listened, and when I'd said my piece, she said, 'Well, we'll see.' And then two days later, your daddy was back." She shakes her head. "Hard to tell."

I try to picture it, but it's not easy to see Mama carrying on inside that big yellow house. That Miss Precious must stand a full head taller than Mama. "How long was Daddy gone?"

ays," Mama says. "He came back on

d he say?"

Mama blinks. "He said he forgot his way home." She smiles a tight smile. "He had a lot of funny stories. We got over it."

I look away. I figure she doesn't want me to see her eyes tearing up. "You want me to help you get Kenneth Lee into bed?"

She nods her head toward the bedroom door. "There's a little cot in the corner in there. You know that?"

I shake my head. I reckon that cot's what Miss Precious meant when she said two beds.

"You go on to sleep," she says. "I can get him in okay."

I pull my green blanket from the pile, stand up, and go on into my little room. Spread it on the floor and lay down. There's a little breeze coming through the window. I never knew that about Daddy going off for ten days. It's been ten months this time. That's a big difference. I reckon it'd take more than some funny stories for Mama to get over it this time.

"Freddy James," Mama whispers through the door. I'm so tired I don't answer. "Freddy James," she says in a flatter, firmer voice.

I roll over. "Ma'am?"

"Next time Johnny comes into town, we could get him to bring in your bed."

"Don't do that," I say. "I'm fine." Johnny Tower's

done plenty for us already, and besides, we're in town now. I'd just as soon keep it separate, the farm from town. Less confusing that way.

I close my eyes. Lick my lips. I still got a taste for that double-chocolate devil cake. Christmas is seven months away. Maybe we won't have to wait that long. I've got a paying job. We might have one for Thanksgiving, and maybe even for next Easter, too.

Next morning I'm up before the sun. Out the door in ten minutes. Couple of houses down I find an alley that cuts through to Main Street. I'm not worried about being late. Fenton's Fine Establishment's probably not even opened up yet, but I'd like to be the first one there. Waiting outside for the door to be unlocked. That'd look good for the first day.

I run out onto Main Street and catch sight of Miss Precious's big yellow house. Setting way up on that hill, looking down on everything else in town, it puts me in mind of that Mount Olympus I read about, where all those Greek gods lived. I didn't have much use for those characters. They helped you out if it suited them, but then they'd turn on you in a second, for no reason at all. If it was me, I'd just as soon take care of my business myself.

A dog jumps up, starts barking, and sets me back to running toward Fenton's. I pull on the front door, and it opens right up. So much for being the first one here.

The only person I see is that same loud redheaded woman from the other day, sitting back in that same corner. She's not laughing now. She doesn't even look awake, except that her eyes are open. Puts me in mind of a fish.

I slip into the room off to the left. There's a bunch of tables and a couple of booths. Metal clangs in the back.

I peek through another door. Kitchen. A colored woman rolls out biscuit dough. "Ma'am?" I say.

She looks up sharp, but smiles when she sees me. "What you need, son?"

"I'm Freddy . . . uh, Fred," I say. "I'm here to see Mr. Calhoun."

"You the boy?"

"Yes ma'am." I reckon I am.

"I'm Dorothea." She indicates a dark hallway with her thumb. "Go on through there. Watch your step."

"Thank you, ma'am."

"Mmm-hmm." She wipes her floury hands on her apron and reaches up above her for a pan.

I watch my step, but the way seems clear enough to me, except for a couple of kegs off to the side. To the right there's a door half open. "Mr. Calhoun?" I knock. Nothing. I push the door open a little farther and squint around. Look down. There he is all spread out on the floor. What looks like blood dried up on his cheek. I move one step closer. And on his chin. Down his shirt a bit. Blood. I'm thinking I'm nothing but a stranger in this town. I'm thinking the smartest thing might be to set out running again.

I'm thinking I've done moved my mama to town, all on account of this man giving me a job, and here he lies, dead. I take another step. Nudge his shoulder with my foot. Real gentle.

Fenton Calhoun's eyes pop open. He blinks. Puzzles up, like he doesn't know who I am or why I'm here. Truth is, that scares me even more than him being dead, the idea that he might have forgotten about me.

"Mr. Calhoun," I say. "It's me. Fred."

He pushes up on his elbows. Blinks again. I take a step back. I sure hope he didn't notice my foot on his shoulder. He shakes his head. Stretches his eyes wide open. Puts his hand on the seat of his desk chair and pulls up into it. Settles back. Frowns. "What time is it?"

"Getting on toward seven." I touch my own cheek. "Are you all right, Mr. Calhoun?"

He rubs some of the dried blood off his face. Looks off past me, like he's looking off into last night. It comes to him. Laughs. Shakes his head. Turns his eyes back on me. "You here to work?"

"Yes sir."

"Well, good, son. There's plenty to be—" Mr. Calhoun doubles over, holding his stomach. "Go get Jacob," he says. "My medicine."

I set off running back down the hall to the kitchen. I smell biscuits cooking, but I don't see the woman.

"Whoa, boy." This tall guy, a colored man, catches me by both arms before I bang into him. "Where you off to?"

"Mr. Calhoun," I say. "He's real sick. He—"

His face wrinkles up. "Sick?"

"He's all doubled over. He needs his medicine. He said to get Jacob."

Smiles. "Oh." Shakes his head. Jabs at his chest. "I'm Jacob." Nods me toward the refrigerator. I follow him. He takes down a big glass with a handle. "Now you remember," he says. "Not one of the little water glasses." Jacob opens up the refrigerator, pours in some milk, and holds the glass under one of the three silver pumps on the counter. Barely touches it. Chocolate blurts out. "Just a half squirt, mind you. Not a touch more."

I nod.

Jacob stirs slowly. "You got all that?" He picks it up and looks at the bottom of the glass. "Don't leave any syrup on the bottom." Gives me the glass. "Mr. Fenton, he hates that, leaving syrup on the bottom."

"Umm."

"Don't keep him waiting now. He hates that even more."

"This is the medicine?"

"For his ulcer." He narrows his eyes at me. "You are Fred, aren't you?"

I nod.

"Well, then, this is your job now."

I stop in my tracks. "Whose job was it before?"

Jacob laughs. "Like I said, it's yours now and welcome to it." Claps his hands. "I got myself a railroad

52

job." Nods his head at the door. "I'd move it if I was you."

"Thank you," I say. Hurry on back down the dark hall.

Mr. Calhoun's turned on a light on his desk. He's still holding one hand on his stomach, but he's straightened up. He holds out his other hand.

I give him the milk.

He takes a drink. "Aaaah." He leans back. Takes a longer drink. Nods. "Jacob show you how?"

"Yes sir."

"I got a hole in my stomach, son. You see that look on my face again, just go to it. Don't ask. Just go."

"Yes sir."

"Now this is the main course of business, as far as you're concerned. I'm digging a barbecue pit out back." He rubs at dried blood on his face. Chuckles. "Jacob's packing for Savannah, but you got to get him to take time to show you what's what out back." He looks at my hands. "You chop wood?"

"Well, sure." Any fool can chop wood.

"Go on then. Jacob'll get you started." He closes his eyes.

I clear my throat. "Mr. Calhoun?"

One eye opens.

"I need to know . . . we best discuss the details of . . . what I'm to be paid, and—"

Opens the other eye. "I figure forty cents an hour's fair. As many hours as you can work, I can use you."

Forty cents an hour. At maybe ten hours a day. That'd be four dollars. Doesn't sound bad.

Fenton drums the desk with his fingers. "Well?" Chuckles. "You reckon you can get by on that?"

"It's not what it's worth," Big Kenny always said. "It's what you can negotiate." And anyway, I don't figure on just getting by. I figure on holding a little back. Who knows how long this job's going to last? Who knows what's coming up next? I figure to be ready for the next surprise.

"I was thinking more like seventy-five cents an hour, sir."

Mr. Calhoun smiles that little half smile, like when he first felt the blood on his face. "Let's just say forty-five."

I open my mouth to say fifty, but he holds up his hand. "Or we could just make it a flat twenty dollars a week."

"No sir." I like the idea of by-the-hour pay better. "Thank you, sir." I nod. "Forty-five's good." At least for now. I back out the door.

Mr. Calhoun nods. Turns off the light on his desk. Closes his eyes.

Seven

Jacob pushes open the screen door beside the sink. "Come on out here," he says, "and I'll show you the operation." His voice is still friendly and slow, like before, but his hands are in a hurry. Galloping away on his leg.

The smell of those biscuits fills me up. I can't move.

"Go on. Get yourself one." Jacob's left foot starts tapping. "And a piece of meat."

I never seen so much ham in one place. Sliced thin. Hot. Curled at the corners. Puddling up with juices. Laying out on the longest pan I ever did see.

"Go on." Jacob's voice is picking up some speed.

I slide the meat inside the biscuit. Follow him outside. Make a business of it. Three bites. I forgot to eat anything this morning.

"Okay," Jacob says. "You familiar with pit barbecue?"

"I've seen pigs done on chicken wire, in the ground."

Jacob nods. "Same principle." He pulls a few folded

pieces of paper from his pocket. Smooths them out on a hickory round. "Look here."

I kneel down to get a good look. Boxes and numbers marked off in pencil.

"This is my plan," he says. "For the pit itself, you got to go down five feet." He points to an area on the far side of the shed.

I follow his finger and nod.

"With this dry spell, that ground's pretty hard. Might want to hold off until after the rain." He looks up at the sky. "I expect we'll get some come Thursday." He shuffles that paper under the next one. "Once that's done, go on to the cage." Shakes his head. "Chicken wire's too flimsy for this operation. I got steel pieces cut already, out in the shed, and this here tells you how to put it together."

I nod.

"You understand it?"

I nod.

"There's canvas out there, too. You cover the pit with it while you're cooking. Hold it down with rocks." Jacob raises his eyebrows.

I nod. "I've seen that." I have.

Jacob straightens up. "If it works out, Mr. Fenton might go with permanent doors, but—" He folds the papers and gives them to me. "Door plans are there, too." Walks over to the woodpile and picks up a piece out of the little already cut stack. "When you're not doing anything else, cut wood. And not bigger than this piece here." I nod.

He looks at me hard. Shakes the wood. "The size of the wood is the difference between—" Shakes his head. "I've seen many a sad barbecue."

I take the wood. Look it over. Nod.

"I'm not just running off at the mouth here." Jacob holds on to that hard look. "Keep in mind the simple things." He takes the piece of wood back from me. "The quality. The size of the wood." He shakes his head. "Too many people get caught up in the . . . in the extra." Nods toward the hole. "It's all nothing without the right wood."

"Yes sir," I say.

Jacob cuts his eyes at me. Grins. "Uh-huh," he says. "Mr. Fenton, he says you're to help me clear out my room." I follow him back inside. The kitchen's still empty, but it sounds like things are picking up out front. Through the door to the bar I see four men dealing a deck of cards.

"You play cards?"

I shrug. "A little poker." That's a lie, but I reckon a man ought to play poker. I figure to learn. "Rummy." Mama can teach me. She's always after me to learn how to play with her and Kenneth Lee, but sitting around and playing with cards always seemed like a waste of good time to me. Leastways, I ought to get her to go over the rules.

"Your daddy—" Jacob shakes his head. "He's a cool number, he is."

"Yes sir."

"He could lose one, two, three hands, stay just as collected, never even the slightest touch of red on his ears." He leans down and whispers, "Not like some of these fools." Pulls back up. "Then he'd come back and win big." Opens up his arms. "Big." Sighs. "Of course, often as not he'd turn around and lose big." Laughs. "That's what he always said, you know, 'Jacob, at least I lost big,' and I'd say, 'Yes sir, Mr. Johnson, you sure did.' " Jacob guides me into his room with a hand on my shoulder. "It's your daddy that kept after me to stop just talking about the railroad and to go on down there. 'Do something about it.' That's what he told me." He smiles. "So I did. And here I am. A railroad man." Shakes his head. "Yeah, I always liked Big Kenny."

I nod. Everybody liked Big Kenny. I've seen him make a grown man laugh until he cried, and even though I never saw him play cards, he was always making wagers over one thing or another out at Art Crenshaw's barn. Over pool and horseshoes and prize fights on the radio. I remember a few times them betting on which of the fellows could run the fastest. It always just seemed like good fun. I never thought so much about the losing before. Or even the winning. I never thought much about the actual money involved at all. All I knew about money is that we never, ever had enough of it.

Jacob taps a black train trunk setting on his bed. "Soon as my ride gets here," he says, "I'll need you to help me carry this out."

I like Jacob's room. Tight and cozy. Off to itself. I wouldn't have minded staying here, if the situation had been different. I pull up one end of the trunk. "What have you got in here?"

"Just my belongings," Jacob says. "It's the picture frames that make it so heavy."

"Pictures of what?"

"You know. My mama. Family."

"Your mama live around here?"

"My mama's dead. Daddy, too."

I don't know what to say.

Jacob kneels down and looks under the bed, but he keeps talking. "This is a good job for a boy just starting out, Fred. Mr. Fenton'll do you right, but"—he laughs—"it's like your daddy told me, he said, 'You're not a boy anymore, Jacob.' " He nods. "He was right." Straightens up. "Now your daddy never did make it into the war, did he?"

"No," I say. "He wanted to, but—"

"That's the gospel truth," Jacob says. "He talked about that war all the time." He pulls on a piece of the floor. "Look here." The plank's been cut out, so it comes right up. He pulls out a handkerchief, full of something—money, I figure—tied up in a bundle. "There's a right big space in here."

I look in. It is.

"You can use it, if you want." He looks at me. "Mr. Fenton says you're renting from Miss Precious."

I nod. "Me and my mama and my brother."

"Uh-huh." Jacob fusses with his bundle. "Of course, now, Mr. Fenton might be renting this room out." He shakes his head. "I been staying here a long time." He opens up the trunk and sets the bundle in there. "No telling what Mr. Fenton might do." He changes his mind and sticks the bundle down in his pants pocket. It bulges out something awful. "Go on out back," he says, "and look for a black pickup."

I race down the hall and see four black pickups parked out back. One of them, though, has a colored lady at the wheel. She waves at me. "Get Jacob," she says.

I run back in. I notice Jacob's bulge is gone. Wonder where he hid the money. I know better than to ask. We struggle down the hall, one of us on each end of that trunk full of pictures, and slide it onto the back of the truck.

"Go back, roll up the mattress, and sweep out the room."

I nod.

"Don't forget what I told you."

"I won't."

He climbs into the truck and closes the door. "Because first time you fire my baby up, I'll be back. I'll be checking up on you."

Jacob and the lady drive away laughing big, happy,

on-the-road laughs. To get to Savannah, they have to cross over a state line, too. They turn to the right and disappear. Truth is, right off, I can't remember a thing Jacob told me. I stand for a few minutes, just recollecting and putting it in the best order I can. I head on over to the spot he·pointed out to me. At least I'll never be at loose ends, looking for something to do. I can always dig. I can always chop wood.

I pull out Jacob's plans. I had listened hard to every word he said, but it takes me awhile to make sense of them the second time. I like that Jacob. I know I just met him, but all the same, I already miss him being here.

Eight

Jacob kept a neat toolshed. I find a tape measure, some nails and string and measure off the spot according to his paper. Force the shovel down around the edges. Darn near shatter my shoulder. Jacob's right. The ground's too hard. I keep at it, though, for a while. Scrape a couple inches off the top before I give up and move on over to the woodpile. You can always chop wood.

Jacob was right about Daddy, too. It was the gospel truth. He sure had wanted to get in on the war. He even went into town once and signed up proper, but then time he got home he found out Aunt Crayton had taken a turn for the worse. She'd been living with her second cousin for the past several years, but Mama and Daddy thought she ought to come back to the farm so we could take care of her.

Daddy's own mama died when he was just a baby, so Aunt Crayton had stepped in and done all the things a mama does. Then, when Daddy was just twelve, his daddy—who would have been my grandpa—up and died from the influenza. So Uncle Cecil and Aunt

Crayton just took Daddy in and raised him like he was their own boy. When Uncle Cecil died, he left the farm to Daddy. Daddy always said it took him by surprise. "Not that there was anyone else left to take it on." He shook his head. "It was too much for Aunt Crayton by herself." He shrugged. "I reckon I just thought Uncle Cecil would be around forever."

"Big Kenny never really took to farm life," I heard Mama tell Minnie Tower, "but I know he thought the world of those two."

Daddy wasn't about to walk out on Aunt Crayton, no matter what was going on over in Europe, not as long as she was on her deathbed. The army seemed to understand. They gave him a dispensation or a delay, something like that, so that he didn't have to go in until after Aunt Crayton was dead and buried. Except Aunt Crayton didn't die. She didn't ever get much better, either, but she hung on until after V-E Day.

"I think it's just her way of keeping you home, safe and sound," Mama said.

Daddy didn't smile. He didn't think it was funny. Not one little bit. Knowing Aunt Crayton, and the way she carried on over Daddy, I couldn't help wondering if Mama wasn't right.

And anyway, it wasn't just Aunt Crayton. It was one thing after another. There was the drought. Then that hailstorm that beat the roof right off the barn, and we had to deal with that. Before we knew it, the war was over. Daddy missed out on it altogether.

"So how's it going out here?" Fenton steps out the back door. Folds his arms. Looks around. He can't be too impressed.

"Ground's pretty hard," I say.

Fenton nods. "Be easier after some rain."

"Yes sir," I said. "I expect we'll be getting some Thursday."

"Got the woodpile going, though." Fenton looks at his watch. "Why don't you knock off now. Get back bright and early in the morning. I got some stock to be put up."

"Yes sir." I gather up the shovel, ax, and splitter.

Fenton slaps his cheek. "Mosquitoes already," he says. "That's a bad sign."

A truck barrels around the corner. That loud red-haired woman is driving and pulls right up in front of Fenton. He doesn't even blink. Just gives his feet a lingering look, walks around, and opens up her door. "About time you got back." Runs his hand along the truck's fender.

"Fenton, I do truly appreciate it." She climbs out. Kisses him on the cheek. "You should have seen my girl. She's grown a mile."

Fenton nods. "You know Evelyn, Fred?"

"No sir." *Evelyn.* "Not really."

"If you don't remember anything else in this life, Freddy James," Big Kenny told me, "remember a person's name, and you're halfway there every time."

Snapped his fingers. "Remember the wife and kids, and you *are* there."

"Well"—Fenton laughs like he's cutting a big joke—"watch out for her. She's trouble."

Evelyn's got a giggle like scratched metal. Beside her Minnie Tower would sound like a fairy princess.

I smile back at the both of them. "Yes sir."

Evelyn smacks Fenton on the arm. "Don't be saying that." She winks at me. "I am not trouble." She winks at Fenton. "Thanks again."

Fenton nods. Looks over at me. "Put those tools away," he says. "I'll give you a ride home." Sounds good to me.

Fenton doesn't have much to say. Just drives. I don't care. I lay my head back against the seat and let the hot breeze blow in my face.

I part wanted Daddy to go to war, and I part didn't. I knew it was the right thing to do. But I knew, too, that they could have killed him over there. A couple of times, though, over in Art Crenshaw's barn, some fellows back from the war started telling their adventures, and I could see how it bothered Daddy. Could see it in his face.

Mama was right. Nobody told a story like Big Kenny. And when he missed out on the war, he got cheated out of a big one.

Fenton jerks the truck onto River Street. I sit up straight. Maybe that's why Daddy left. He was shipping out. Just like he meant to all along. It wasn't his fault they ended the war up too soon. Maybe he thought he could still get in on the tail end of it. He should have said good-bye, though—at least to me. Mama might not have understood about the war, but I would have. He ought to have known that.

"What's that Fenton Calhoun got you doing all day," Mama asks.

"I'm supposed to be digging a barbecue pit, but the ground's too hard." Jacob was wrong about the rain being on its way. We've gone almost a week without one drop. "I wash a lot of glasses."

Mama nods. "Plenty of drinking going on, I reckon."

"And sweeping," I say. "And putting up stock."

"Stock?" Mama pulls her hands out of the dishpan. Turns around. Gives me that narrow-eyed look. "What kind of stock?"

Mama keeps asking me questions like she thinks Fenton's up to something. Maybe he is. There's a lot going on over there that doesn't have anything to do with me. "Nothing much," I say. "Milk, eggs, and whatnot. Just the essentials."

That's what Fenton calls his little grocery shelf out front. He just keeps the "essentials" on hand, he says, for "the boys that don't have any women at home to take care of them." Just crackers and canned goods and eggs, but I bet he makes a right smart of money off those few little things. He charges way more than they do down at the grocery.

I pointed that out to him, how anybody could buy his goods cheaper over at the grocery, and he said, "Yeah, Fred, I charge a fair sight more than the grocery." He picked up an egg out of a flat. "You know why?"

I shook my head.

"Because I can." He held the egg up between his thumb and index finger. "Convenience, Fred," he said, "is just as much a commodity as this here egg. Man's hungry at the end of the night, with no woman at home looking after him." He shook his head. "He's not at the grocery store, and even if he was, chances are it's closed by the time he notices he's hungry." He set the egg back down in the flat. "People'll pay for convenience, Fred, just as sure as anything else."

Convenience. I reckon he's right about that. I've seen a couple of fellows there that eat by just sliding raw eggs down their throat. Buy them by the flat and keep them in the trunk of their car. Just crack one open when they get weak from not eating. I've seen them do it. Right on their teeth. Dorothea says they keep so much alcohol in their system, their stomachs can't handle much else.

A pretty pathetic way of living, but I reckon that's their business. And I guess it's Fenton's business to give them what they need.

After supper I sit with Mama out on the back steps. You can hear Susannah talking French back and forth with a couple of her ladies. Kenneth Lee digs up a strip of ground alongside the house.

"Isn't that ground too hard to dig right now?" I ask. We'll be getting some rain tonight for sure. You can smell it.

"Nope."

"What are you up to?" Mama asks him.

"Nothing." He sure is intent to be up to nothing. He looks up at Mama. "How long you reckon we'll be staying in town?"

Mama looks at me. Shakes her head. "Don't know." She leans against the railing and closes her eyes.

I feel a bit of drizzle. Stand up. "I'm going on in," I say.

Mama nods. Doesn't open her eyes. "Good-night, Freddy James," she says.

I hold out my hand. "It's starting to drizzle."

Mama opens her eyes. Looks down at Kenneth Lee struggling with his shovel. "We'll be right along." She takes my hand. Squeezes it. Lets it go.

The rain comes down light and steady, cools my room down, and I drift into the best night of sleep I've had since we came to town.

This morning I don't even bother with the front door. I run right around back and get out the shovel.

Dorothea pokes her head out the kitchen door. "Mister Fenton wants you back in his office, Fred."

I run on back to his office. "Yes sir?"

He points toward the front. "That wind kicked up a mess out front last night." Fenton's hair stands up every which way on top. He rakes it down with his fingers. Looks like he just slept in here last night. "Get that cleaned up first, before you get started out back." He squeezes his eyes shut. Opens wide. Moves them around. "That's what you're getting at? The pit?"

I nod. "Yes sir." Maybe he sleeps here every night. For all I know, Fenton lives here. I go on out front. It is a mess. A trash can's rolling around over on the other side. Banging against the wall. That's the culprit. Might be the wind that kicked up the trash, but more than likely it was some drunk that started it all. Knocking the can over on his way home.

It takes me the better part of the morning to get the trash all picked up. Finally, I get to start digging. The rain pounded down the lines I'd laid out. I get down on my knees and mark off the space again. If Jacob wants to come back and measure it, he can. It'll be perfect.

"Fred."

I look up. Dorothea's got her black patent-leather pocketbook on her arm. She's going home. "Yes ma'am?"

She gives me two ham biscuits wrapped in a napkin. "And go in and get yourself some milk, boy." She shakes her head. "And you ought to be wearing a hat out in this sun."

"Yes ma'am." I stand up. "Thank you, ma'am."

"Uh-huh." She straightens her bonnet.

"See you tomorrow, ma'am."

Dorothea nods and heads on down the dirt road toward the tracks. She has another job, cleaning somebody's house, two days a week.

I finish off the biscuits. Duck inside the door and take a dipperful of water. Get back to work. Takes me less than three hours to dig the whole pit, now that I got some soft ground to work with. I'm down in the hole, patting and smoothing the sides when Fenton steps out and calls me.

"Down here, sir."

Fenton walks over. Looks down. "Good Lord a'mighty." He shakes his head. "Be careful you don't work yourself right out of a job, son." Kneels. Reaches down. Gives me a hand up. Jerks his head back. "Come on," he says. "I got some business. We best go ahead and settle up now."

I follow him back to his office.

Fenton sits down behind his desk. "Way I figure," he says, "you put in about forty hours this week."

I run that through my mind. Eighteen dollars. "I figured I was here more like forty-five, sir."

Fenton laughs. "You figured, did you?"

I nod. I intend to from now on.

"Okay then." Fenton figures right on his desk, on the wood, with a pencil. Opens up a metal box. Counts out three fives into my hand. Drops a quarter on top.

I look at him.

Fenton laughs. "You are a quick one." Shakes his

70

head. "I'm taking out enough each week, to cover the rent, to pay up Miss Precious."

I'd just as soon have the whole amount in my hand. To deal with Miss Precious the way I see fit. I open up my mouth to say just that, but it's like Fenton reads my mind. He holds up his hand. "This is the way it is. You don't want to get on the wrong side of Miss Precious." He stands up. "Well." Holds out his hand. "I'm happy," he says. "How about you, Fred."

I take his hand. Hold it tight. Three times. Up and down. "Yes sir," I say. "I'm happy." I hold out one of the fives. "Except for, do you reckon I could have five ones instead of this bill."

Fenton laughs. Waves me away. "Ask Paulie. He's got some ones behind the bar." Pulls the chain on his lamp.

"Yes sir," I say. I figure Mama ought to be able to get by on twelve dollars. I'll hold back three. And keep the quarter for pocket money.

Nine

Fenton needs another storeroom, so I've stayed late every night this week cleaning out that room next to his office. I figure it's been fifty years since somebody's been through that junk. I'm hot, sore, and hungry, so once I get all the shelves nailed up today, I cut out for home a little early. I'll move in the boxes piling up in the hallway tomorrow.

"Nice as could be." I'd know that screechy voice anywhere. I slip my hand off the screen door handle and listen. "Even Johnny said so. But they had papers. Told him he'd best be on his way." Minnie Tower.

"Papers?" Mama's voice is a whisper. "What kind of papers?"

"I don't know." Minnie takes a noisy sip of something. "But Johnny said they were serious papers. He drove back over, on Thursday, to get the chickens, seeing as how he'd already made that deal for you, to sell them to the Clinkscales." Minnie's voice goes low, too. "But they were gone. And the cow, too. Out of the barn."

"You know," Mama says, "I looked high and low, but I never could find that deed."

Kenneth Lee barrels up behind me. "What you doing?" He pushes past.

"Watch out!"

He pulls open the screen door and runs into the kitchen. "Mama!" he yells. "Look what I got from Miss Tinsley across the street."

I follow him in. With all this commotion, I might as well.

"What?" Mama winks at me. "You boys say hello to Mrs. Tower."

"Hey," I say. "Good to see you."

Kenneth Lee nods. "Tomato plants." He holds out three scraggly little seedlings. The weak ones that you have to pull out to make way for the healthy ones. Weeds. That's what he's all worked up about.

"Can I set them out? You think there's enough sun there by the steps?"

Mama laughs. "Do *you* think there's enough sun?"

Kenneth Lee jumps up and down. Dirt drops off the spindly roots, onto the floor. "Yes ma'am."

"Then I'll have to go with your judgment on that."

He bounces back out the door.

"So how's Mac doing?" I sit down at the kitchen table. "And Mr. Tower?"

"Same as always," Minnie says.

"Minnie was nice enough to bring us our mail." Mama stands up and walks over to the table. Lowers her voice.

"There's some cornbread on the stove. And a little milk's left." She points over by the sink. "And a couple of sliced tomatoes." Rubs her hands together. Raises her voice. "I know Minnie won't mind if you go ahead and eat some supper." She shakes her head. "That Fenton works him like a dog."

Minnie nods. "You go ahead and eat, honey." She points her finger, arching her wrist up, with that way she has, over to the other side of the counter. "And when you're done with that, you have yourself a piece of my apple bread."

"I already had a piece myself." Mama smiles at Minnie. "It's as good as always." She goes back over and sits down beside Minnie.

I take down a bowl. Put in two pieces of cornbread. Pour what's left of the milk over them. Mash the cornbread down. Look up at Mama. "Mail from who?"

Mama shakes her head. "Just business." Smiles. "And a letter from your Grandpa Sullivan. I'll read it to you boys tonight." She turns back to Minnie. "So anyway," she says, "I did talk to that Miss Hennie Crenshaw, over at the dress shop—"

Minnie claps her hands. "And she's giving you a job."

"Well, no," Mama says. "She said she needs someone to take in her laundry, and she knows some other ladies . . ."

The smile falls off Minnie's face. "Well"—she takes Mama's hand in hers—"be careful of your hands. Nothing ruins your hands like laundry." She shakes her head.

Mama laughs, but neither of them looks happy. I used to find it right funny listening to Mama and Minnie carry on, but tonight they just make me sad.

A horn blows out front. Twice. Loud. Minnie jumps up. "That's the Petersons." She looks over at me. "They gave me a ride in."

"Say howdy for me," I say.

Mama walks with her to the door. "Thanks for everything, Minnie."

Minnie shrugs her shoulders. "Johnny didn't know what to do. We just thought you ought to know."

Mama rubs her arm. "I'll walk you down," she says.

No sooner do Minnie and Mama move down the front stairs than Susannah Doolittle eases in through the door from her stairs. I wonder if she was just waiting behind the door. Listening for when they left. I might do something like that, but it seems strange for a grown lady like Susannah Doolittle to not just walk in whenever she's good and ready.

"And how are you this evening?" Susannah opens up the refrigerator. Takes out a plate with a boiled egg and some cheese on it.

"Fine, thanks."

Kenneth Lee runs in the back door. "Where's Mama?"

"Out front." He races past us.

"Kenneth Lee?" Susannah says.

He stops short. Turns around. "Yes ma'am?"

"That book suit you?"

He breaks out into a big goofy grin. "Yes ma'am."

Nods. "Thank you." Turns and bolts down the front stairs.

Susannah sits down across from me. Laughs. "That boy's a pistol."

"What book's that, ma'am?"

"*Three Musketeers.*" She sprinkles a little salt on her egg. "I let him borrow it."

"He been bothering you?"

She shakes her head. "No. He's a good boy." Cuts her cheese with a knife. I'd spend my whole life at the table if I was as careful with my food as Susannah Doolittle. "Your mama's friend, she's very pretty."

I shrug. "I guess so." Flashy, that's the word Big Kenny used for Minnie. I'd go with flashy myself, before pretty, but I reckon a lady might be both.

Susannah smooths her hair back. It's up in a bun today. "She's got pretty hair." Opens her hands out wide. "So much of it."

I shake my head. "That's just the sugar water," I say. Susannah's eyebrows shoot up. "Pardon?"

"Sugar water," I say. "And snuff cans." I hold out my thumbs and fingers. Roll them back and forth. "You know." I think back to how Mama described it. "The sugar makes it stiff."

Susannah nods. "Makes the curl stay put." Smiles. "That's a good idea."

I shrug. "But Minnie's hair's not naturally blond, you know. It's peroxide."

Susannah laughs out loud. "You're a regular jack-of-all-trades, aren't you, Freddy James?"

I blink. I don't get it. "Yes ma'am." I reckon I am.

Susannah wraps back up the bit of cheese she didn't finish. Stands up. Takes her plate over to the sink. Turns on the water to wash it. "You fix hair, too, do you?"

I gasp. "No ma'am. I just heard—"

She laughs. I've never seen her laugh so much at one time.

Mama comes back in. Sits down at the table across from me. "Kenneth Lee's putting in some little tomato plants out back," she says to Susannah. "You don't mind, do you?"

"Not as long as he shares his harvest."

Mama smiles, but it doesn't look like she much means it. She looks at me. "You get paid today?"

I shake my head. "Tomorrow," I say. "Fenton said we'd settle up tomorrow."

"Bye now," Susannah says. "I got a student coming."

Mama waves. Nods. "Tomorrow." Straightens up. "Did you hear what I told Minnie? About taking in laundry?"

I push away my empty bowl. Look at her. "We out of money?"

Mama shakes her head. "We can get through tomorrow, I reckon." Swats at a fly buzzing around her head. "Would have been plenty, except that I had to buy some new T-shirts for Kenneth Lee." Lowers her voice.

"Those others were riding up over his navel. Some kids laughed at him."

"Mama!" Kenneth Lee calls from out back.

She stands up. "Have yourself a piece of Minnie's bread. It really is good." Pats her pocket. "Come on out back when you're ready, and I'll read you Grandpa Sullivan's letter." Opens up the screen door. "What do you want, Kenneth Lee?"

I wish Mama hadn't run out of money, but she's trying to rub it in with the cornbread and milk. We still got beans we brought with us. She could have cooked up a pot of those. She'd probably say beans aren't any good without a piece of salt pork, but they fill up your belly just the same.

I'm not saying I don't feel bad. Sitting here with three folded dollar bills stuck down deep in my pocket. But it's just one day. We'll get through that. Mama said so herself.

Grandpa Sullivan says in his letter that he bets I'm growing into a fine man. He asks about Kenneth Lee's hijinks. He tells us about Grandma Sullivan winning a blue ribbon for her plum preserves, even though he already wrote us about that once, back in the fall, when it happened.

"Your grandma made him put that in." Mama rolls her eyes. "She wants to be sure not any of us forgets it."

Kenneth Lee's still down poking around in his new

garden. He looks up. "How come Grandma doesn't ever write to us?"

"She used to." Mama holds out her hand. "She has a touch of the palsy now." Shakes it. "Makes it hard for her to write." Looks back down at the letter. "Of course, she could if she really wanted to. She just used to be so proud of her beautiful handwriting."

"What else does Grandpa say?"

She shakes her head. "Not much."

I look over her arm. There's more. "What?"

Mama pulls her lips tight. Then reads. "I can't believe it's been eight years since we've seen you and Kenny and the boys, Eleanor. I can't imagine any other life but farming, but it sure gets a grip on you, stronger than a snapping turtle, every day of every season of every year. I know you're grateful for your land, just the same as us, and I know you're tied to it, just the same as us, but, Eleanor, I sure hope to see those boys again while they're still boys."

Kenneth Lee's kneeling down. Only half paying attention. I catch it, though. "Didn't you write to Grandpa about us moving into town?"

Mama folds the letter. Slips it back into her pocket. "That's pretty much it." She leans back against the railing.

"Maybe," I say, "Grandpa hasn't gotten your letter yet."

Mama looks at me. "I didn't tell your grandpa about moving into town."

"Don't you think you ought to tell him, in case—"

Mama leans into me. Lowers her voice. "No," she says. "You don't know everything about everything, Freddy James. Your grandpa wouldn't think moving into town was such a great idea. He'd think leaving the farm behind was the same as leaving a living member of the family behind. That's how he thinks." Tears puddle up in her eyes. She squints to keep them in. "He'd think it was just shameful. Just as shameful as it was for Big Kenny to walk out on us." She reaches out and grabs my arm. Squeezes it hard. "But you know what, he'd find a way to twist that around to make it my shame." She lets go of my arm. Jabs at her chest with her finger. "Mine." She sniffs.

I don't say a word. I'm sorry I brought it up. I'd be mad at her for carrying on like that, except for that three dollars down in my pocket. I feel guilty.

She wipes her eyes. Kenneth Lee sits on the bottom step. Gives us a quizzical look. "I'll let him know in good time." Winks at Kenneth Lee. "Soon as we get our feet solid on the ground." Nods at me. "We'll go down there and tell him ourselves. In person."

It's Mama that put it in my mind to hold some money back in the first place. That night after she finally admitted Daddy was gone, after she sat around and talked to us about growing up in Saultee, she sent me and Kenneth Lee off to bed. Nothing ever keeps Kenneth Lee awake.

His head had just barely hit the pillow before he was making those wheezy sleeping noises of his. I was about to drift off myself, but a chair scraping across the kitchen floor snapped me out of it. Sound of glass clinking around. I got up and went to the door. Mama was stepping down off the kitchen counter, onto one of the kitchen chairs, with a coffee can in her hand.

She didn't see me. She sat down at the table and pulled out wads of dollar bills. Flattened them with her hand. Poured out the change. Stacked the coins. She counted to herself, moving her lips.

"Mama?" I said.

She jumped. "What are you doing up?"

"Where'd you get all that money?"

She shook her head. "It's not all that much." Waved me back into the bedroom. "Just what I've managed to hold back."

"Oh."

She pointed her finger at me. "And where would we be right now if I hadn't?"

I went back to bed. She seemed to think I had a quarrel with her, but I didn't. I was happy to know we had that little bit of money. I did think about going for six weeks with a hole as big as a fifty-cent piece in my one pair of shoes, when all the time I bet she had enough money in that can to buy me four pairs of new shoes if she'd wanted to.

So I'm not saying I wouldn't have thought of it on

my own, but the idea did come to me direct from Mama. Not just the idea of holding back, but the idea that it ought to be secret.

I leave the three dollars in my pocket, fold my pants, and push them under the pallet when I lie down for the night. If Mama was to find that money and ask me what I was holding back for, I'd say, "Well, where would we be now if I hadn't?" Three dollars poorer, that's where. She couldn't argue with that. Cornbread and milk for supper suits me fine as long as I can go to sleep with three dollars under my head. You never know what's coming up next. And tomorrow, after I get paid, I'll sleep even better with six dollars.

Ten

Fenton comes out back and walks around the barbecue pit. "So," he says, "you reckon it's done."

I been working on the cage all week. I kneel down. Pull on it. Tight as a drum. I'm proud of my part, but truth is, it's Jacob that did the real work, drawing up the plans. All I did was the labor. "Yes sir," I say, "unless, of course, you want to go with the doors."

"You could do that?"

"Yes sir." I shrug. "Jacob pretty much had a plan for everything."

Fenton rubs his chin. "I'm still working on the sauce with Dorothea, but this is how I figure it. We give it a trial run on the Fourth."

Two weeks from Friday. "Yes sir."

"We work the kinks out over the Fourth, then we kick off the whole operation full-time, come Labor Day."

Full-time. I glance over at the woodpile. We're not even using it yet, and already I'm chopping wood a couple of hours every day. Of course, Fenton won't ever pass up the opportunity to sell a load. "You mean have it going every day?" Hard to imagine cutting wood full-time. I work my shoulder around, just thinking about it.

Fenton kicks at the woodpile. Looks it up and down. Looks at me. "Well." He smiles. "Maybe we start off weekends, see how it goes, roll into full-time." He winks. "The best things in life"—he rolls his hands around, one over the other—"you just roll into." He points over to a black pickup parked in the shade. "Before you go," he says, "hose down that truck." Shakes his head. "Don't have to detail it, just clear off the dust and clean the wheels." He squeezes his eyes shut. Winces.

I jump up. Run into the kitchen. Reach up for one of the big glasses. Fill it with milk. Half squirt of chocolate. Stir. Check the bottom. Stir a couple more times, just to be sure. Run back out to Fenton.

Fenton presses hard into his stomach with one hand. Takes his medicine with the other. "Thank you, son." Drinks half the glass down. Takes a deep breath. Looks over at the woodpile. "And be sure you fill that out a little before you go."

I take on the pickup first. Sweat's pouring down the back of my neck. I've been looking for a reason to turn on some water.

That first week I was here I kept trying to match up people with vehicles parked outside, but I kept coming up short on the people side. Then one afternoon I saw a fellow lose bad in a poker game and pay up with his green Chevrolet. Left Fenton's walking. Couple of days later another fellow showed up at Fenton's walking, money changed hands, and he drove away in the green sedan.

"Not my main order of business, the cars," Fenton told me. "Just one of my sidelines." He didn't seem to pay much attention to the buying and selling of cars. There just happened to be, one way or another, two or three vehicles for sale out beside Fenton's. If you were interested, you knew where to go. But he did like to keep them clean. Maybe he wouldn't care as much, though, if he had to wash them himself.

Anyway, if Fenton could just settle on one order of business around here—didn't have so many sidelines— he might not have that hole in his stomach. At least that's what Dorothea thinks. She doesn't put much stock in his chocolate milk remedy. "Nothing but nerves," she always says. "If Mr. Fenton would just settle down, that problem would take care of itself."

When I finish washing the truck, I go in and wipe down the kitchen. Dorothea gets mad as the dickens if she comes in and finds the counters messy. I do what I can.

Then I go on out and get started on the wood. It's almost supper time. By all rights, I could go on home, but I don't mind. Fourth of July. It's pretty exciting to have a definite plan to finally fire up the barbecue pit. And I know it's a definite plan, because Fenton didn't just tell me. I heard him talking up the Fourth of July barbecue with some boys in the pool room. It's going to happen. I know that much about Fenton. Once he's spread it around the pool room, he won't change his mind.

Up until then, though, I was beginning to wonder. Fenton might call all that fussing with Dorothea working out the perfect sauce, but I just call it silly. All I've heard from Dorothea is how she makes a perfectly fine vinegar, brown sugar, and tomato sauce, and how it's served her people good enough for five full generations. And all I've heard from Fenton is his nagging about that mustard sauce he had down in Columbia. Dorothea says a little bit of mustard is okay, but she doesn't know anything about any full-blown mustard sauce, and she's not interested in learning about it now.

Fenton offered to drive her down to Columbia to try it, but Dorothea wouldn't have any of it. She just turned around and walked away. Threw up her hands. "Mustard." She spit the word out, like it's the stupidest idea she'd come up against in a long time.

I like mustard. All I've ever had is tomato barbecue, but I'd like to get down to Columbia and to at least try it. Big Kenny always said, usually when he was trying to get finicky little Kenneth Lee to eat, that a man's got to be open to new things.

What I'd really like to do is come up with my own money-making plan. Draw it up and figure it out on paper like Jacob, but be able to stay with it from start to finish. And to be in charge. If I wanted mustard to be a part of it, it would. I'd see to that.

Come the Fourth of July at Fenton's, though, I figure we're going to be having regular old tomato sauce. I don't see Dorothea budging on that count.

I overdo it on the wood. My muscles feel about as solid as pudding. I put away the ax and splitter, and instead of walking on home, I go in and take a seat at the bar. I don't know if Paulie's being funny, or if he's just as tired as me and not thinking, but he pours me a beer instead of giving me a Coca-Cola.

There's one other fellow at the bar. An old man. And Mitch and some of his type are at the table behind me. They're all knocking back their beers. My whole body's sticky from the heat. Those beers look cool and foamy and just plain right. I pick up my mug.

"Whoa." Paulie laughs. Realizes what he's done. "You much of a drinker, Fred?"

"On occasion," I say. "Once in a while." Everybody looks.

"Oh Lord," Mitch says. "If there's anything worse than those once-in-a-while drinkers"—he looks around at the other fellows—"it's the beginners." He looks around. Laughs and winks. Just like Custis Fullbright.

That tears it. I was set to slide the beer back and get my usual Coca-Cola. Or maybe let it go warm, slip it down the drain, and go on home for supper. But Mitch throws his two cents in, and I'm suddenly in no hurry to go home. I take a good long drink. I'll show him.

It doesn't go down easy—I won't say that—but I don't cough. That's what's important. That I look like I know what's what. The second sip doesn't go down any easier, but it goes longer, and just the plain wetness of it hits the spot. I can feel sweat running down my neck in little dribbles. I'm thinking about me sitting here drinking a beer, just like the rest of the boys, and about how the pit's finally going to be fired up, and I'm not in such a hurry to get home.

"Bucky!" A guy yells out from Evelyn's usual corner table. Evelyn's gone this week, visiting her little girl who stays out at her mama's, from what I've heard.

I'm about to take my third sip, trying to make a business of it, but I look up to see this tall fellow strut through the door. He's got blond hair and looks like a picture off the cover of a magazine. Like a war hero. Like a pilot. Like Odysseus finally making his way home from that Trojan War. A cut above these other characters. You can see that.

"Would you look at that," Mitch whispers. "Bucky Kent."

Bucky Kent. I've heard of him. One night I was laying in bed, trying to get to sleep, but Mama and Susannah Doolittle were talking in the kitchen. Talking about the war.

"Well, Eleanor, you know as well as any woman that some people made out, and made out big, on that war, and they loved every minute of it," Susannah said.

Mama didn't say anything I could hear. I knew she

was thinking about Daddy. About how he missed out on it.

"Why," Susannah said, "I don't have to look any farther than Bucky Kent. All my life Miss Precious tells me I'm going to Europe, but look at who really goes. Bucky Kent. Thank you, Miss Precious."

"Bucky Kent," Mama says. "That was your fiancé?"

Susannah laughed. "It never quite came to that."

"I'm sure," Mama said, "that Miss Precious meant what she said. Nobody could imagine a man like Hitler coming along."

"Well," Susannah said. "I can't see why not."

"But surely things are so you could go to Europe now, wouldn't you say?"

"The time," Susannah said, "is past." That tone of voice of hers just altogether settles whatever it is you're talking about.

That's the first time I heard about Bucky Kent, but his name always makes an appearance in Susannah's stories, one way or another. She never lets out any actual facts about him. Just spits out his name with the same feeling other people put into saying "Adolph Hitler."

Bucky Kent bypasses Mitch's table. I like him for that. He sits down at the corner table. Mitch and his boys get up. Go over and stand around behind him. The old man at the bar goes, too. "What you doing in town, College Boy?"

I stay at the bar, but I listen up. Bucky Kent lives over in Tennessee now, and goes to this college called

Vanderbilt. He was in the war, just like I figured, because he starts in telling some story about France. Most of them, they've heard the story before, that's plain enough, with the way they jump all over his sentences.

I look down. I can't believe it. My beer's gone. Paulie's over with the others, listening to Bucky Kent. I ought to be cooling off, but sweat's just pouring down my neck. I go behind the bar. Open up the box. No Coca-Colas. A few of those Buffalo Rock Ginger Ales. Mama's crazy for those, but I'd as soon eat fire as drink a Buffalo Rock. I pour myself another beer. Take a sip. It feels cool in my mouth, but doesn't do a thing for my neck. I move to the back. Into the crowd. I'm just calling attention to myself sitting over at the bar alone.

They're all leaning and whispering and laughing into one another now. I can't follow what they're saying. Fenton comes out of the back. Pulls up a chair.

Paulie kicks into action. Collects empties. Takes them over to the bar. Disappears into the back. Comes back with a case of Coca-Cola. Fenton hates an empty box.

"Hey!" Mitch pulls Bucky Kent up by his collar. Draws back his fist.

Bucky Kent shakes free. Looks down at the guys. Shakes his head. Laughs.

Fenton stands up. Jerks Mitch back, but not before he pops Bucky a shallow one. "Fool," Fenton says.

Bucky Kent opens up his arms. "That's just what I said." He laughs. There's a little spot of blood in the corner of his mouth.

Fenton pulls Mitch over to a far table and sits him down. Points his finger. Puts me in mind of a teacher putting a rowdy kid in the corner. Pretty stupid.

I'm light-headed all of a sudden. I drop onto the only open chair. Fenton's. He slaps me on the back. "I thought this was your supper time, Fred."

I lose my grip on my mug. Catch it quick, though, with my other hand. "What's wrong with you?" Fenton takes the mug. Smells it. "Oh for . . ." He pulls me up by my arm and leads me down the hall, past his office, to Jacob's room. "Lay down," he says. I do. He closes the door. The room goes black.

I jump up out of a dream. One where we're all sitting around a big round table. Eating mustard barbecue. Daddy's telling war stories. Everybody's listening. Laughing. Slapping their legs.

My head hurts. My mouth's dry. I'm hungry.

Bucky Kent's lathered up, leaning up against the mirror. He's got that little glass lamp turned up toward his face. "I wake you up?"

"No." I blink. "What time is it?"

"Morning." He scrapes the lather off the other side with his razor.

"You staying here?"

He shakes his head. "I've just got to clean up a little before I see my mama." He splashes his face. Dries off. Hands me a Coca-Cola. "Want this?"

He's like one of those Greek gods. Of course, in

Odysseus's case it was a woman, the goddess Athena, that always showed up just at the right time. She might take on some confusing form—like as not she'd look like a man—but if Odysseus knew what was what, she'd give him what he needed to get through the next day. I take a good long sip of Coca-Cola. Sure hits the spot. "Thank you," I say.

"So." He leans in close to the mirror. Checks out that cut in the corner of his mouth. Didn't amount to much. "Fenton tells me you're staying over on River Street with Susannah."

"Well," I say. "Upstairs." I reach in my pocket. My money's still there.

"How's she doing?"

I glance down at Jacob's secret spot on the floor. "Just fine." I'd thought about hiding my money in there, but I think I better come up with something else. A second-hand secret spot doesn't strike me as particularly secret.

"She ever mention me?"

"Now and again." I wiggle my toes. My feet are cramped from sleeping in my shoes. "Something about you running off." I finish my Coca-Cola. I could use another one.

"I don't think I'd call it running off." He dabs a little piece of newspaper on a bloody spot on his chin. Looks like he's done more damage with a razor than Mitch did with his fist. "I went into the navy."

"You going over to see her then?"

Bucky steps back from the mirror. Cuts his eyes over

at me. "Okay," he says, "maybe I did run off." Smooths the front of his shirt. "But not because there was anything especially wrong with Susannah." Looks at me. "You like her, don't you?"

I sit up. "Yeah." Susannah Doolittle's been nice enough to me, so I'm not altogether comfortable with this conversation.

Bucky nods his head. "Well, you should. And I reckon it's true what everybody says about old Miss Precious." He laughs. "Good as gold." Slips on his jacket. "Generous"—he cuts his eyes at me—"to a fault."

I stiffen up. I'm sure not about to comment on Miss Precious. Not to some stranger like Bucky Kent that just up and appears out of nowhere and starts up talking. I don't know him.

He holds up his thumb and index finger. Less than an inch apart. "I came this close to marrying Susannah Doolittle, and Miss Precious was sure ready to help out. She'd give us a house. Give me a job. Send me to school first, if that's what I wanted." Shakes his head. "Gave me the creeps after a while. That old lady, she owns the whole town. She's got to own me, too?" Shivers. "No thank you." He picks up his comb. Sticks it in his jacket pocket. Looks at me. "When you first met Susannah, what did she say? Who'd she tell you she was?"

I thought about it. "Susannah Doolittle," I say. "Miss Precious's adopted daughter."

Bucky Kent snaps his fingers. Points at me. "Exactly. Miss Precious's *adopted* daughter. What's that?"

I shrug. I don't know.

"I tell you what it is. It's a lack of commitment. On the one hand"—he slings his left arm out—"Miss Precious's daughter, part of all that money and power." He slings out his right arm. "But on the other hand, not really. *Adopted*. Not *really* a part of the whole Miss Precious empire." Nods. "You see? Both ways. Susannah Doolittle could have run off, too, but she had to have it both ways." He stops. Moves his tongue around his teeth. "You got any toothpaste?"

I shake my head. "Fenton does."

Bucky Kent winks. "Good enough." Salutes. "See you, kid." Struts out front without looking back.

I sneak out the back door. Sun's high. Mama's going to kill me for staying out all night. I start out running, but the more I think about what I'm going to say, the slower I go. She can't really have anything to say about where I spend my nights. What with me working all the time and being dead tired by the end of the week. What with me paying for that blamed apartment and all this town living she takes to so easy. Can't have it both ways.

I expect to find Mama out back hanging up her laundry to dry, but she's in the kitchen sitting at the dining table. Wearing her good green dress. And her little Sunday hat with the veil. First thing comes to my mind is somebody's dead.

She looks at the door. "Kenneth Lee out there?"

I shake my head. "No ma'am."

She sighs. "I went to see that Miss Precious this morn-

94
○

ing." She's not looking at me directly. Sort of over my shoulder. "Seems your daddy had a fair amount of debt with Miss Precious, seems he owed a lot from gambling, and so he let her hold the deed to the farm until he paid up." Looks me right in the eye. "Seems she sold the farm."

"*Miss Precious* sold *our* farm?"

Mama nods. "Seems it's been her farm to sell for a year now." Taps her fingers on the table. "You got to go back to Fenton's or—"

I nod. "I wasn't working last night, I . . . I was real tired and just fell asleep in the back room, and—"

Mama's not listening. "Better hurry then." She unpins her hat. Takes it off. "It's all we've got now." Stands up. "And I've got a load of laundry to be done and delivered by six."

I wash up, change my shirt, and sit down to a bowl of grits she puts out for me. Mama's changed back into her everyday dress. She runs up a tub of soapy water and dumps a basketful of clothes into it. Doesn't say a word. Doesn't even look at me. Just goes on about her business.

I scrape the bowl clean and rinse it in the sink. "Mama?"

"Hmm?" She rubs the shirt harder.

"Who'd Miss Precious sell it to?"

Her head jerks up. "I don't know," she snaps, "and I don't care." She swipes at a piece of hair slipping out over her ears. "I'm happy I don't have to go to bed every night worrying about what's going on out there, worrying about whether or not we did the right thing. . . ." She sighs.

I didn't even know she was worrying about that. She never said so. Truth is, unless Kenneth Lee brought it up, I never even thought about the farm.

Mama pushes her hands down into the tub so hard that water splashes on my pants. "But I'll tell you who's not happy," she says, "and that's your Great-aunt Crayton."

That hits me hard. "Aunt Crayton?" For a while there I'd forgotten all about Mama's peculiar behavior when Daddy first left. "Mama," I say slowly, "Aunt Crayton's dead."

Her head jerks up again. "I know she is." Her eyes lock with mine. "And, believe me, that only irritates her all the more, knowing Big Kenny's lost her land with her dead in the ground." Mama shakes her head. "Where she can't do a thing about it."

I run all the way back to Fenton's. Truth is, for all my piece I was ready to say, all about Mama and Kenneth Lee being such a burden on me, up until just now, I felt free as a bird. There was always the farm just waiting for us, if we ran into trouble in town. I had it both ways. Not anymore, though. Mama's right. I reach into my pocket and count out the edges of nine folded dollar bills. This is all we've got now.

Eleven

Fenton's down on his knees and looking under this fellow's car. "No." He braces himself against the side of the car and stands up. "That's a bad leak, son." Shakes his head. "Not much of a trade." Nods over at the black pickup I washed yesterday. "Might knock ten dollars off the price." Rubs his chin. "Might could do that."

"No, Fenton." The other fellow's just a kid. Whines like one, too. "That's nothing. Could be sealed up easy." Pats the fender of his car. "This is a good car. I just need a truck right now."

Fenton nods. "Well, if you can fix it easy, fix it on up. Bring it back. We'll see what we can do."

The boy's head drops. "Well, thanks for nothing, Fenton." Goes all sullen. Worse than a two-year-old.

Fenton laughs. The boy speeds away. Fenton was right. His car left a mess of oil on the ground.

Fenton cuts his eyes over at me. Reaches down and wipes the dirt off the knees of his pants. "And how are you feeling today?"

"Fine."

He laughs. "Well, I sure hope so." Nods over toward the woodpile. "I see you got a right smart amount of wood cut yesterday before you started in on your drinking."

I nod. "Yes sir."

Fenton levels his eyes with mine. "Don't try that trick again, son. You'll be getting me into all kinds of trouble." He moves over to the barbecue pit. Kicks at the cage. "You sure this thing'll hold a pig? A *big* pig?"

"Yes sir."

"Okay." Points at me. "I'm taking your word for it."

"Fenton . . ." I sigh. I got plenty of questions. I just don't know which one to start with. So I just tell him something I know. Something to maybe get him started. "Miss Precious sold our farm."

"Yeah," Fenton says. "I heard about that."

"How could she do that?"

"Well." Fenton rubs his chin. "Big Kenny borrowed a lot of money from Miss Precious—a little at a time, the way I understand it—so I reckon the amount just crept up on him." Fenton looks at me. Nods. "That'll happen."

"Yes sir, but—"

"Well, the way I heard it, Big Kenny gave Miss Precious the deed to the farm as what you call . . . collateral. You know what that means?"

I shake my head.

"It means she was giving Big Kenny the chance to come up with the money, but, meanwhile, she was holding on to the farm as . . . insurance." Fenton opens up his hands. "I mean, Miss Precious might be rich, she might be willing to help folks out any way she can, but in the end, she's in business, just like the rest of us."

I shake my head. "No." I don't get it. Owing money, that's one thing. Giving away Uncle Cecil and Aunt Crayton's farm, that's something else altogether. "How much money you reckon she got for the farm?"

Fenton holds up his hand. "You can ask her yourself. She called over here this morning. Wants to see you."

"Me?"

"Yep," Fenton says. "After she talked to your mama." He raises his eyebrows. "How's she taking the news?"

"Fine."

Fenton laughs. "Fine." Snaps his fingers. "Everything's always fine."

"Yes sir." Might as well be. Nothing me or Mama can do to change it.

"Tell you what," Fenton says. "I'll give you a ride." Points to the black pickup. "Let's give that one a go."

It's as if I've been called up before some sort of queen. I think about what Bucky Kent said, about how he didn't want her to *own* him, and then next thing I know she's up and sold our farm. I think about that fellow Susannah told us about that did the work on our apartment. Miss Precious doesn't like how he goes about it, and next thing he knows, he has to go clear out of town to get another job. Miss Precious might not be enough of a queen to throw me in a dungeon or cut off my mama's head or the like, but she could sure do some damage. If she wanted to, she could put us out on the street right now.

"So Big Kenny didn't tell you, didn't tell your mama, didn't tell anybody, about Miss Precious holding on to the deed to the farm?"

I shake my head.

"Well, I got to say this, Fred," Fenton says. "Me and Big Kenny go back a long way, but that was wrong." He glances over at me. "And next time I see him I'll tell him so."

"You think you'll see him?" Those first few weeks after Daddy left, I ran out to the road and looked down after every pickup clattering by, hoping it might be him. Now I don't even know what I'd say if he just showed up in Fenton's one night.

"Never can tell." Fenton slaps my leg. "You know, we're talking whole hog barbecue here, and if that cage don't hold—"

I'm glad he changes the subject. Far as I'm concerned, it's okay for Daddy to just stay where he is for now. "Fenton, I got right down in that pit and stood on the cage," I say. "I figure if it'll hold me, it'll hold a dead pig."

Fenton laughs. Nods. That satisfies him. I haven't *exactly* climbed down and stood on the cage, but I know I could do it. Truth is, if I was to draw up my own barbecue plans, I think I'd go a little deeper into the ground than Jacob, but I know that cage will hold. Just to be sure, though, I'll get down in there today. Just to be true.

"Okay, Fred." Fenton turns the truck into a dirt drive that cuts up the side of Miss Precious's hill. He stops in front of the long yellow porch. "Good luck."

I look at him.

Fenton snaps his fingers and points at me. "I'm just kidding."

I get out. Fenton skids off. Kicks up rocks and makes a terrible racket. I look around, half expecting that old man of hers to pop up and call me over into the bushes, but then I just make myself march right up the steps to Miss Precious's front door. Just like Mama said *she* did.

I raise up my hand, but Miss Precious opens up the door before I can knock. She's wearing a dress today, but she's got on those same ugly men's shoes. She looks down after Fenton's dust. Shakes her head. "Come on in, Fred," she says.

So I finally set foot inside that big yellow house, and this is all I can say. It's not much. It's big, with long, high windows, and that's nice, but otherwise it's just pure ordinary. Common, that's what I think Mama would call it.

"Sit down, Fred."

I sit down in the closest chair. A big red upholstered one. Dust flies up. Swirls around in the sun shining through the window. Roses press up against the window. Miss Precious does have a nice yard. I'll say that.

"As you may or may not know, your mother paid me a visit this morning."

I nod. "Yes ma'am."

"Okay." Miss Precious sits down across from me. Settles back. Folds her arms. "And did she tell you about me selling the farm?"

"Yes ma'am."

"What did she tell you?"

"She said that Daddy owed you money, and that you sold the farm to get your money back."

Miss Precious nods. "Okay." She straightens up. "Owed me money for a good long time now." Leans toward me a little. "You remember when you first came up here, looking for a place to rent?"

I nod.

"You remember what I asked you?"

I shake my head.

"I asked you who sent you. Your mama? Your daddy?"

"Oh, yes ma'am." I nod. "I remember that."

Miss Precious crosses her legs. Even on a man those shoes would be ugly. "You remember what you told me?"

"Yes ma'am. I told you Fenton Calhoun—"

Miss Precious holds up her hand. "Right." Sighs. "But, you see, Fred, I didn't believe you." Folds her arms again. "Given the situation, I figured you or your mama—at least one of you—had to know I had that deed. Why else would you be moving into town"—she unfolds her arms and marks off each word with a shake of her hand—"right when I'm getting ready to collect on my debt?" Opens her arms out wide. Holds them high. Like a preacher. "But you didn't know. You or your mama or the two of you just up and decided to move into town on a wild hair." She points a finger at me. "That took gumption. I'll give you that." She stands up and holds out her hand.

I take it, on instinct, but I'm not sure this is a handshake. I don't make a move. Miss Precious just gives my hand a squeeze. Lets go. "If I'd thought for a minute that your mama didn't know about me having the deed, I would have paid her a visit before I sold the farm." She crosses her arms over her chest. "Other than that, I make no apologies." She uncrosses her arms and folds her hands together like she's about to pray. Presses them against her mouth. I wait for her to start talking again, but she doesn't.

"Yes ma'am," I say.

She moves over, behind a desk. I can see now the room's not the jumbled mess I thought it was when I came in. There's not just the one desk; there's four of them, set up with their separate papers and chairs. More like an office in here than the front room of a big house. It's just not what you expect.

Miss Precious pulls open a drawer. More of that dust flies around. "Now," she says, "I knew Big Kenny since he was a boy, and I always thought he had a lot of promise." She pulls out a long white envelope. "But he has deeply disappointed me." She tips the envelope toward me, but doesn't seem as if she really wants to give it up. I keep still. "He told me that he had a good job in Michigan, and that he would be sending me payments—"

"Michigan?" From time to time I've imagined Daddy in far-off places like California or Europe, but I never would have imagined him in Michigan. I don't reckon I'd even know how to imagine Michigan.

"Factory work's what he told me"—she shakes her head—"but the more I think about it . . ." Gives me a hard look. "Believe you me, I'd much rather have the money in hand—that your daddy promised me—than fool with selling a rundown little farm any day." She sighs. "I couldn't get top dollar. Barely"—she raises her eyebrows—"just barely made back what your daddy owed to me." She fans herself with the envelope.

"How much did you get for the farm, ma'am?"

Miss Precious blinks. "Just barely enough," she says, "to cover your daddy's debt." Her lips pull into a thin, tight smile. "Believe you me, I don't owe this to you"— she holds the envelope up next to her head—"it is a gift." She shoves the envelope right at me.

I take it. "Thank you, ma'am." I don't open it.

Miss Precious closes the drawer with her hip. "I give you this because I sympathize with your situation, because I think you have gumption—" A woman peeks in one of the doors off to the side. Miss Precious nods her in. "And I do have hope that you might behave better in this life than your daddy."

It feels like dollar bills in the envelope. "Miss Precious," I say, "do you think my daddy might be . . . dead? That maybe that's why he didn't get you your money?" I sure don't want him to be dead, but at least it would explain how he let all this happen.

Her mouth drops open. "Oh." She shakes her head. "For heaven's sake, no." She looks up at the woman. "What have you got, Angela?"

This woman, this Angela, she's not all that much older than me. "You asked me to remind you to give him this." She gives Miss Precious a cigar box and hustles on back out the door.

"Oh yes. I meant to give this to your mother. They found some things in the house."

I take the box. "Thank you, ma'am." Seemed to me we left a house full of stuff. "Is this all there was?"

Miss Precious nods. "All that seemed worth saving." She sits down behind her desk. Opens up a drawer. I expect to get something else, but she calls out, "Angela, I need some of that carbon paper in here!" She looks up at me. "Don't dillydally now. Fenton's all worked up over his barbecue."

I reckon she's done with me. I ease on out the front door and down her hill into town. Miss Precious is good as gold, I reckon, like folks say, but still I can see how she got under Bucky Kent's skin.

I duck in behind a big stand of crape myrtles and sit down. It's a good cigar box with roses and black-haired women on top. From Cuba. Everybody says Cuban cigars are the best. There's a few photographs inside. One of Mama's mama, my Grandma Sullivan, standing in front of a rosebush, and another one with her and Grandpa Sullivan sitting in a porch swing. Grandpa's got his arm around Grandma's shoulder, and she's looking down, like she's embarrassed. Mama used to have these stuck on the mirror in her bedroom.

There's one of Daddy standing in front of a brick wall and what might be the ocean—it must be when he was down in Charleston. He's swinging a straw hat around, out to the side of his head, like a cowboy at a rodeo.

I think about what Fenton said to me, that first day in Elderton. "The first time I laid eyes on you, I knew you were Big Kenny's boy." Fenton seeing Daddy in my face was like having Daddy there, making everything go easier.

I think about how Miss Precious smiled when she said, "So you're Big Kenny's boy?" She sure wasn't smiling now. As far as I can tell, all being Big Kenny's boy did for me today was get me on the wrong side of Miss Precious. I wish all these people would just forget about Big Kenny. I wish when they look in my face, they'd just see me. Freddy James Johnson. I didn't run out on anybody. I don't owe anybody any money.

I open up the envelope. It's money all right, but it's

not dollar bills, it's *ten*-dollar bills. Ten, twenty, thirty, forty, fifty . . . eighty dollars!

I look around. Count it again. Ten. Twenty. Thirty. Forty. Fifty. Sixty. Seventy. Eighty dollars. I lean back, slide my hand down into my pocket, pull out the nine dollars I've held back and put it into the envelope with the eighty dollars. I put the envelope in the bottom of the box, under the photographs. Miss Precious said it was a gift. Nothing wrong with that, I reckon. And this cigar box will sure come in handy; I can slide it way back under that low shelf in the corner between the bathroom and kitchen. Nobody will ever know it's there.

I get up. Peek out through the crape myrtles. Nobody. I run all the way home. I've got eighty-nine dollars on me, and I'm plenty nervous about it.

Twelve

Fenton and Paulie are in the hall, sorting and shelving liquor boxes. Fenton nods me into his office.

There's a stack of cardboard squares on his desk. A pot of India ink. A fountain pen and a brush. Fenton wants me to make signs about the barbecue.

Fenton makes out like he doesn't really care what the sign says. "Just make it clear when it is, where it is," he says.

I sit down. Tap my fingers on his desk. Pick up the brush.

"Get it in about women and children! Women and children welcome," Fenton yells through the door.

I lay down the brush. Take a pencil out of his cup and write on a plain piece of paper:

Fourth of July Party
Fenton's Fine Establishment
Real Pit Pork Barbecue
Noon Until ?
Women and Children Welcome

I take it out and show it to Fenton. He says just what I expect him to say. "Just use your own judgment, boy." He says it, but he takes the paper all the same. Looks it over. Holds it between his teeth while he hoists up another box to Paulie. I know then he's got some changes. Just like I figured he would. Fenton takes the paper out of his mouth. "Look here," he says. He spits out some paper that got left behind. "What you think about this?" He's talking to Paulie. Pointing at the word *Party*. "You think some people might take that to mean 'free'?"

"Nah," Paulie says. "People ain't that stupid." Laughs. "Fenton Calhoun giving away free barbecue." Shakes his head. "I don't think anybody'll be expecting that."

Fenton doesn't laugh. Gives me the paper. "Do something with that women and children line." Shakes his head. "Don't know why, but it sounds funny."

Women and children. He's right. It's like what people say when they're jumping off a sinking ship. Women and children first. "How about we say families? For families or—"

"For the whole family." Fenton nods. "See, the Fourth, that's a family holiday." Rolls his hands one over the other. "We got to pull them all in to make a go of this thing."

I spend the best part of the morning making twelve signs, using a ruler to line up the letters. One thing I've noticed is whenever I see a sign with letters all over the place, with words spelled the wrong way, I just don't pay it any attention. I figure, what's that fool got that I want to know about? He can't even make a decent sign. Up in the corner, right past the first line, I even draw in a firecracker with sparkle lines coming off the fuse.

Fenton peeks in. Stands back, on the other side of the desk, like, at least for this little while, it's my office, and he doesn't want to disturb me. "What's that?" he asks, pointing down at one of the firecrackers.

"That's a firecracker," I say. Maybe it doesn't look quite as good as I thought it did.

Fenton laughs. "Nice touch." He picks a sign up and holds it out to look at it. "Nice and neat." Lays it back down. "One end of Main Street to the other. And out at the armory. Don't forget the armory."

Most folks don't care. Don't even look up. "Sure thing," they say, gesturing out front. At the grocery store they've set up a special little community bulletin board, just for this sort of notice. I like that. Thinking ahead. "You just come back by, and pick it up now, when it's out of date." She smells like vanilla. Miss Crawford, I think that's what Mama calls her. Miss Crawford down at the grocery. Anytime Mama passes on some bit of inside gossip about goings on in town, and I ask her how she came to know about it, she'll say, "I heard it from Miss Crawford down at the grocery."

"Yes ma'am," I say. "I sure will." She even has a little box of thumbtacks right there. "Thank you, ma'am."

Miss Crawford pulls her rectangle glasses down on her nose and leans over her cash register. "Fenton Calhoun?"

"Yes ma'am."

"And he's asking over the whole family, is he?" She laughs.

"Aiming to have a big Fourth of July party, ma'am." I look over at her chocolate drops. If it wasn't so hot, I'd get some.

"Aiming to sell a truckload of barbecue, I reckon." Shakes her head. "I never seen the like."

They'd just melt in this heat by the time I got home. "I'll be back, ma'am, to take it down on the fifth."

"Oh, I reckon the sixth will do just fine," she says.

La Dresse Shoppe doesn't look as friendly. When Mama told me she was doing laundry for Hennie Crenshaw, the lady down at the dress shop, I figured Hennie wasn't her actual name. There it is, though, right under the La Dresse Shoppe. Proprietress, Hennie Crenshaw. It's not only her real name. She's proud of it.

As soon as I open the door and smell that fancy Minnie Tower–type smell, I wish I'd just kept walking. A fairly normal-looking lady checks herself in a tall mirror over in the corner.

"Can I help you, young man?" The tall skinny lady who speaks to me, though, is not normal looking at all.

"I wondered, ma'am"—the lady in the corner turns around and listens, too—"if I might put up this notice in your window."

"In my window." She takes a paper from me. She's noisy, what with the gold and silver jewelry hanging off her, and the rustling of her shiny—taffeta, satin, silk, I don't know what you call it—stiff green dress.

"Yes ma'am." I try not to look directly at her.

"Fenton Calhoun!" She drops my sign. Stomps on it with her matching shiny green shoes. "That home wrecker!" She points to the door. "I should say not."

"Ma'am," I say. "It's for the whole family, this barbecue, for the Fourth of July—"

She pushes those white shiny glasses up on her pointy nose. "You work for Fenton Calhoun?"

"Yes ma'am."

She looks over her shoulder at the woman at the mirror. "He's just a boy."

"Miss Crenshaw." That's just a guess, but I figure it's a good one. "Please. I'll stick it right down in the corner."

She sighs. Stoops down and picks up the paper. "I'm sorry, young man—"

"I'm Eleanor Johnson's boy, ma'am." I take the notice from her. "That does your wash."

"Oh." She sighs. "Very well." Shakes her head. "Down in the corner."

It looks good there. A lot of ladies are bound to see it and, for whatever reason, that's important to Fenton. I reckon Miss Crenshaw must like Mama well enough. There's not one other notice in her window.

Now Cooper's Drugstore is another story. His front

window's cluttered up with every notice from the last ten years, far as I can tell. I know it won't take any talk to stick one in there, but then I wonder if it's worthwhile to get caught up in all that mess. It isn't a matter of being too nice; that grocery store lady, she's nice, but she has a system. You need a plan, you need convenience, and you need a system. That's just good business.

But then I'd hate to just walk on by. Feels like I wouldn't be doing my job. I squint through an open crack, between a War Bonds poster and some butter-and-egg man's notice. That red-haired girl is behind the soda fountain. A chocolate soda, that would go down real good right now.

I got two quarters in my pocket for spending. I try not to consider the fact that I've got all that money hidden away in the cigar box. I don't feel guilty about holding back money and not telling Mama, just as long as I don't touch it myself. When it comes time to touch it, I'll know, and then I'll tell her about it. Even if I decide I got to take that money myself and run off, I'll tell her first. Just too much confusion comes from the other way.

Besides, Mama knows I keep a quarter or two in my pocket. She wouldn't hold an ice-cream soda against me. First off, though, I take care of business.

"Sure thing, son." Mr. Cooper's in back with the medicine. "Some of those notices might be out of date." He waves his hand. "Just take something down, if you have to."

Might be? I got to laugh. It would take a body two days to go through all those pieces of paper. I take down the sloppiest one. Didn't even check it for a date or anything. If you don't know how to make a proper sign, you ought not have the right to stick it up in public. It's Mr. Cooper's fault; he ought to have a system.

An old white-haired lady pushes open the front door. Squints around the store. Smiles at me.

"I got you fixed up back here, Miss Caroline," Mr. Cooper calls out. "You watch your step now."

Miss Caroline looks over to the fountain. Waves at the red-haired niece.

"Howdy do, Miss Caroline," she says.

Miss Caroline laughs like she's cut some kind of joke, and heads on back for her pills. I jump down off the window ledge. Head over to the soda fountain and take a seat. The red-haired niece has her back turned, leaning over the counter, reading a magazine. "Ma'am?"

She looks up and laughs. "You talking to me?"

"Yes ma'am," I say. "I'd like a chocolate soda." I lay a quarter down on the counter.

"Okay." She closes the magazine. "You want chocolate or vanilla ice cream with that?"

"Vanilla." I hadn't thought about it coming any other way.

She went to work, squirting syrup with one hand, soda water with another. "Next time," she says, "you just order a black and white. That's what it's called." She scoops a big portion of vanilla that hangs off the side of the glass. Sets it on a plate. "See how it sets up on the glass so nice?"

I nod. "Thank you—"

"Don't call me 'ma'am.' Okay?" She smooths out a napkin and lays down a long-handled spoon. "My name's Roberta." She steps back and smiles at her soda. "It's called a lip, that flat part there." She points. "Without that it just plops right over in the soda, it spills down on the saucer, makes a mess . . ." She nods her head back toward Mr. Cooper. Lowers her voice. "That's how *he* makes them."

"I reckon they taste just as good, though."

Roberta rolls her eyes. I get started on the soda, seeing as how the lip's slipping. The ice cream's bound to fall into the soda at any minute. I can see she wouldn't like that, and I can see she's the type that would probably make it out to be my fault. After a minute or two of getting that under control, I say, "So Mr. Cooper, he's your uncle?"

"Was he talking about me?" She stands up real straight and folds her arms over her chest. "What did he say?"

"Nothing." I clamp my mouth down on the straw. It's not as if I even care whether he's her uncle or not. Just talking to be polite. This Roberta could use a few lessons on being polite herself.

Her head jerks up. She's done with me. "I'm watching you, you little thief!"

I turn around. Kenneth Lee. We lock eyes. I jump up. He runs out the door. I bolt after him.

I drag Kenneth Lee home by the collar. He's kicking and yelling and hanging on to a wagon. It rattles along and bumps up into my legs. "Where'd you get that wagon anyway?" Kenneth Lee, he doesn't make words. He just yells. Calling attention to himself. Big baby.

He breaks loose in the backyard and runs up the steps calling out for Mama.

I'm right behind him. "She called him a thief."

"And who is this *she*?" Mama's at the sink washing up some dishes. Kenneth Lee's all red-eyed and hanging on her waist, but he's putting on. Mama doesn't even turn around and look at me.

"Mr. Cooper's niece, that works the soda fountain at the drugstore."

Mama turns around now. "That mouthy little red-haired girl?" Kenneth Lee sticks his lip out and rubs his finger on his mouth with that way he has. "*That's* who we're talking about?"

"That girl wasn't even talking to me, Mama." He cuts his eyes over at me. "She was talking to Carlton Smith. You know Carlton." He pulls on Mama's sleeve. "I told you about him."

Mama nods. "And I told you not to be hanging around with him."

"I wasn't!" Kenneth stomps his foot. "He was there when I came in."

"Then why did you run out the door like that?" That's what I want to know.

Kenneth Lee's eyes bulge. "Because you jumped at

116

me like a crazy person!" He wails at Mama. "He scared me."

"That's stupid." I got to laugh. "Who is this Carlton Smith?"

Mama shakes her head. "Into everything, from what I hear."

Kenneth Lee waves his hands around. "He's that blond boy, standing over next to the candy, who that girl was yelling at!"

I do remember a boy like that. Over next to the candy. Maybe that *was* who Roberta was yelling at.

Kenneth Lee narrows his eyes at me. Slumps off into the front room and opens up that book Susannah Doolittle gave him. I reckon he really does like it.

I sit down at the table. "Where'd that wagon come from?"

"I bought it off those people down the street." Mama squints. "The Thomases. The Thompsons. Something like that." She pours the water off of the potatoes. "Kenneth Lee uses it to deliver my laundry."

I didn't know she was doing so much laundry that she needed a wagon to make deliveries. "Mama, I might have been wrong." It's best to just move on. The whole episode's left me confused. I meant to do the right thing. "She might have been talking about that other boy." And I left behind half an ice-cream soda. Just wasted it.

Mama nods toward Kenneth Lee. "Might want to tell him that."

"He hears me." Kenneth Lee pretends like he's reading, but he's grinning from ear to ear. I've said all I'm going to say. "What's that smell?"

Mama opens the oven. "Look at this, boys." Pulls out a brown-roasted chicken.

Kenneth Lee runs in. "Chicken?" Mama gives him three plates. He throws them around.

"Susannah Doolittle bought it." Mama tears off the legs and slices off the breast meat. "Said if I'd cook it, we could have half."

"Is she going to be eating with us?"

"No," Mama says. "She has a student." She places one of the legs and some of the slices on a piece of wax paper. Wraps it. Gives it to me. "Put this in the refrigerator."

I take it.

"That's more than half," Kenneth Lee says.

"No," Mama says, "it's not." She sets the chicken on the table with the potatoes and cornbread. There's field peas, too.

"Where'd you get those?" I love field peas.

Mama slices her square of cornbread down the middle and slides in a pat of butter. "Bought them off a truck, down by the armory."

Kenneth Lee's trying to stay down at the mouth, but sulking and eating don't go together too well. He moves on, too. At least for supper.

"Susannah's having a tea," Mama says.

My mouth's full. All I can do is nod.

"You ever heard of that? A tea?"

I shake my head.

"It's a quiet, fancy little party. You have them in the afternoon."

"Sunday?" I wipe my mouth with my napkin. Lay it back beside my plate.

Mama reaches over and puts it in my lap. "Thursday," she says.

"Thursday?" I sop the last of the peas with my cornbread. Mama thinks I eat too fast. She's always saying that. "Most people . . . don't they have to be at work in the afternoon?"

"Well, this party's for the ones that take her French lessons." Mama forks me over another slice of chicken. "And, as a matter of fact, Susannah asked me to make a dessert for this tea." She laughs. "She wants me to make my double-chocolate devil cake for this tea."

A double-chocolate devil cake. In June.

"She says she'll pay me. She says that if I bake cakes as well as I make regular food, I might be able to sell them around, at the diner and whatnot." Mama pours herself another half a glass of iced tea. "Of course, I wouldn't take Susannah's money."

"I reckon you would."

"She's been awfully nice. I wouldn't feel right."

"Would we get some?" Kenneth Lee reaches over for another piece of cornbread.

I shake my head. "You want to throw in a second cake, fine, but you got to set the price. Make her know what it's worth."

119
◦

I remember that week I hired out to work for Hoyt Axel. "You got to set the tone," Daddy told me. "If you don't set the tone from the beginning, they got you."

"No," Mama says. "She made a point of it, that she would pay me, but . . ." She shakes her head. "I don't know. Maybe thirty cents." She looks at me.

"What if she has another one of these . . . these . . . ?"

"Teas," Mama says.

I nod. "You got to set the tone from the beginning, so you know what's what." I run all that sugar and cocoa and butter and eggs through my head. "More like sixty," I say. "Fifty would be rock bottom, I'd say."

Mama grins. "Maybe I'll just trade her a cake for a French lesson."

I look at her. "I reckon." As long as she gets something.

Kenneth Lee bounces up and down in his chair. "Can I go outside."

Mama holds up her hand. "In a minute." She looks at me. "About that other business . . . earlier."

Kenneth screws up his face at me. I roll my eyes up to the ceiling. I'm over it. We're over it. It's in the past.

"We're going to be okay, boys." She reaches to us. We all hold hands. I suddenly think maybe we're about to pray.

Kenneth grins. "We're going back home."

Mama sighs. "No." Cuts her eyes at me. She thinks we ought to hold off telling Kenneth Lee about the farm.

I think she's right. "Not right yet." She squeezes my hand. Leans in. "Between your work over at Fenton's, between the laundry and"—she winks at Kenneth Lee—"between Kenneth Lee making my deliveries"—grins—"maybe now with my double-chocolate devil cakes, we're going to be okay." Squeezes again. "But only as long we stand up for each other." She moves her head lower. Tries to make me look straight in her eyes. "No matter what."

"I guess." It's working so far, but it sounds like we might be getting into too many sidelines. Like Fenton.

Kenneth Lee cocks his head and yells, "One for all, and all for one, that's our motto!"

Mama blinks. "What?" Lets go of my hand.

Kenneth Lee swings his fist in the air. "That's what the Musketeers always say."

"Musketeers?"

"In my book."

Mama nods. "Musketeers." She grins. Reaches up and grabs his fist. "One for all . . . ?"

"And all for one!" Kenneth Lee crows like a rooster.

I shrug. Go ahead and put my hand up there with them.

Mama grabs it. "There you go." Winks at me.

Thirteen

Some mornings at Fenton's are like a morning's supposed to be. Like the start of a brand-new day. Other mornings are like this. Like the tired, smelly dead-end of a long, hard night. You just never know.

Mitch is over behind the bar, on the phone. His hair hangs down in his eyes. Fenton sits back at the corner table, leaning against the wall, with his hands behind his head and his eyes closed. I head right back to the kitchen. Fill a big glass with milk. Give it half a squirt. Stir it, scraping all the chocolate off the bottom.

Dorothea's kneading her biscuit dough. Gives me a nod. "He'll be needing that," she says.

"Yes ma'am." I've seen some respectable women, who wouldn't be caught walking through the front door of Fenton's Fine Establishment, sneak around back to buy a dozen of those ham biscuits off of Dorothea. Fenton says it's the ham biscuits that keep the place from going under in the lean times.

I set Fenton's glass on the table. He opens his eyes.

Rocks his chair down. Drinks the milk. Shakes his head. Slides a napkin over and snaps his fingers. "Get me a pencil," he says. There's a cup of them over at the end of the bar. "Okay," he says. He writes down a name. "You know that boardinghouse, the one Old Lady Koone runs?"

I shake my head. "No sir."

"Two-story white house," he says. "Over by the mill."

I nod. "Yes sir. I've seen that."

"Well"—he hands me the napkin—"this fellow, this Sam Davis, he stays over there, and I think he might be out of work right now."

"Yes sir."

"Try him first." Fenton calls over to Mitch. "You get through?"

Mitch hangs up the phone. Shakes his head. Rakes his hair out of his eyes, but it falls right back down.

"Try him for what, sir?"

"Hmm?"

"Try this Sam Davis for what?"

"Oh." Fenton chuckles. "Just tell him Mitch needs some riders. Him and anybody else he knows." He holds up three fingers. "We need three."

"Three . . . riders?"

"Right." He waves me on. "Don't worry about explaining it, Fred. If they look at you like they don't know what you're talking about, just move on. We don't want them."

"Yes sir." I look at the napkin. Sam Davis. I knew a boy back home named Sam Davis. Fairly common name. I think I can remember that. Mitch needs a rider. I reckon Sam Davis will know what I'm talking about.

I reckon. Already I don't like the tone this day's taking. Yesterday and the day before that, everything Fenton had me do was about the barbecue. Today, it's like he's just moved on to a whole new idea.

Miss Koone's boardinghouse could use a good going over. Paint and new screens and whatnot. I knock on the front door. The top screen pops out of the frame. If this Sam Davis is out of work, it looks as if he might find plenty of odd jobs to do right here.

"Yes?" A right tall old lady comes down the hall, wiping her floury hands on her apron. She stoops and squints at me. Shakes her head. "We're full up here, son."

"I'm Fred Johnson, ma'am, here to see Sam Davis on business."

"Business?" She snorts. "Monkey business, I reckon."

"Mitch needs a rider." I say it just to see if it makes sense to her.

"Beg pardon?" She unlatches the screen door. "Sam!" She looks up the stairs and yells. "Fellow here to see you." She shakes her head. Chuckles. "On business." She disappears down the other end of the hall.

"Yeah?" Sam Davis stands up at the top of the stairs.

His hair sticks up. His belt hangs open. His T-shirt's pulled up over his belly, and he's scratching.

"Sam Davis?" I ask.

"Maybe." A pack of cigarettes is rolled up in his right sleeve. He pulls the pack out. Gives it a shake, so that just one cigarette slides out. Strikes a match on his pants. Lights the cigarette and puts it in his mouth. Squints at me. "What you got?"

"Fenton sent me," I say. "Mitch needs a rider."

"Just one?" He pulls down his shirt. Rubs his eye with his finger. "Who else has he got?"

I shrug. "He needs three all together."

He stretches out his arms with one hard move. More of a jerk. Comes down the stairs toward me. "What about you?"

"No sir." I take a step back. He rolls his hand in and out of a fist. I've seen that before. That fist reflex. You see that in a fellow, you best take a step back. "Fenton just wants you and a couple of other guys."

His hair falls down over his eyes. He pushes it back up with the cigarette hand. Squints at me. "Who are you?"

Miss Koone comes out of the kitchen, pulls her apron off, and hangs it on a hook. "Don't be giving the boy a hard time, Sam." She put her arm on my shoulder.

"I'm Fred Johnson," I say. "I work for Fenton."

Sam Davis rubs his flat belly. Smiles. His teeth are straight. I expected them to be all crooked like Mitch's. All the same, I like this man even less when he smiles.

He tilts his head back. Looks at me from that angle. "Tell Fenton I'm in. Tell him I'll try to get Carl. I'll be on over later."

"Yes sir." I nod at Miss Koone. "Ma'am." I push open the screen door.

"You need a drink, son?"

"No ma'am." I run on over and give Fenton the message.

Dorothea's working late today, fixing up one of her pots of chili. She sets me to work chopping onions and tomatoes while the beans simmer. "So Fenton's pulling cars again?"

Pulling cars. So that's what's going on. "I reckon he is," I say. I've heard of that. "What does that mean exactly?"

Dorothea stirs up a bowl of cornbread batter. "Means he pulls cars from up north, fixes them up down here, then resells them." Pours it up into a black pan. "Mitch—he's the driver this time around—he drives up north, up to Buffalo, New York, and thereabouts, picks up on some rusted-out cars cheap, then he and his riders—about three or four of them—drive those cars, pulling one or two along in tow behind them." Dorothea rakes my onions into the pot. Fries them up with some green pepper.

"How do they find so many rusted-out cars?"

Dorothea pours in the tomatoes. "You find them on every street corner up there." She pushes around with her wooden spoon to break up the tomatoes. "With all that snow they get, they have to put salt out on the roads."

"Salt?"

Dorothea nods. "Seems the salt melts the snow." She shakes the spoon and lays it across the top of the pot. "But the problem is, that salt gets up inside the car bodies and just eats them up with rust."

"Just regular salt?"

Dorothea nods. "If we ever get ourselves another snow, you try it for yourself." She drains the pot of pinto beans. "A car's body don't last for nothing up north, but I've heard, as a rule, they've got fewer miles on them than what you find down here." She pours the beans into the simmering tomatoes. "Keep that stirred around," she says.

"Why's Fenton go to all that trouble for rusted-out old cars." There was another time Daddy disappeared. I'd clean forgotten about it. Maybe five years ago. Except that he didn't really disappear; Mama knew where he was all along. You could tell that. I thought maybe he'd sneaked off from Aunt Crayton and gone on over to Europe to fight in the war. When I told Mama that, she laughed at me. Set me straight. "He'll be back in a few days," she said. "He's pulling cars. We need the money." That's where I'd heard about pulling cars. I'd clean forgotten it until just now.

Dorothea jerks her head toward the pot. I reckon I'd stopped stirring. I start up again. "They pull some pure pitiful-looking vehicles down here," she says. "And they pull out some pure miracles on this end." She drains the hamburger meat and pours that in. "Leastways, they used to. When old Pinson died, who used to do their body work, Mr. Fenton carried on like it was the end of the world." She opens up the oven and checks out her pan of cornbread. "They seem to think this Lawrence boy, though, that he'll be able to fix them up nice."

"So Fenton'll put them out with the others." If four guys come back with three cars each, that would be twelve more vehicles for me to keep clean.

"Maybe a couple of them." Dorothea laughs. "They'll run most of them to Columbia or maybe up to Charlotte to sell."

"How come?"

She pulls the cornbread out. "They look good at first, but"—she shakes her head—"time will tell."

Dorothea says Mitch gets a cut from the riders for taking them on, and the riders get a cut for the cars they bring down. I'm not clear on whether the body guy, the Lawrence boy, gets a cut or if he's just paid outright.

"What's Fenton's part?"

"Turn that heat down a bit." I adjust the flame. She leans down. Looks at it. Nods. "Mr. Fenton, he gets a cut just for being Mr. Fenton, same as always." She cuts the cornbread into squares and digs them out onto a plate. "You want that ragged piece?" she says.

"Yes ma'am." I'm glad it's an end piece; Dorothea's crust is the best. "They run okay, don't they?" Maybe I ought to save up and buy one myself. Mama could use it to deliver her laundry.

Dorothea nods. "Long as you know those good looks won't last, long as you know what's what, you can make yourself a good deal." She nods toward the door to the bar. "Peek out there and see how many's at the table with Fenton."

Sam Davis has showed up with his fellows. Fenton's going on to them and Mitch about what to look out for up north. Everything from cracked universals to wicked women. It's interesting that Daddy pulled cars—I'd like to hear his opinion about the whole operation—but I sure hate to think of him being a part of that sorry group of fellows.

And I'm not sure what to make of that idea of taking the cars out of town to sell them. I figure it's up to the buyer to know what's what, and it's up to the seller to get as high a price as he can. That's just good business. But I figure if you've got to take your business out of town, you must be doing more than making a good deal. You must be tricking folks. I don't hold with that.

"Okeydokey, then," Dorothea says. "Spoon me up five bowls of that chili." It only takes Dorothea a second to throw the bowls around the table. She doesn't like it one little bit when Fenton asks her to stay on longer than usual. "Spoon yourself up a bowl, if you want."

I reckon I will, seeing as how I've spent the whole afternoon cutting and chopping for it.

"You like it?" Dorothea scrapes off the crust left around the edges of the cornbread pan.

"Yes ma'am."

She looks at me. "So now who you think knows more about barbecue sauce? Me or Mr. Fenton Calhoun?"

"I'd have to say you, Miss Dorothea." I clean another bite off my bowl with my spoon. "I don't reckon I've ever eaten anything Fenton's cooked." I take my bowl over to the sink and wash it.

Dorothea slaps her hand on the counter. "Now that's the gospel truth! I reckon if he knows so much about it, he can do his own cooking." Nods her head. "That is the gospel truth."

"I guess I'll run on home now, Miss Dorothea." I don't want to hear any more of this barbecue sauce business. I'm sick and tired of it.

"Me, too, son." She smiles. "My grandbabies'll be wondering why I'm not along." She pulls her apron over her head.

"Miss Dorothea?"

"Mmm hmm?"

"Your grandbabies ever ask where you are . . . when you're over here working for Fenton?"

"My babies always asking after me, Fred. I need to bring them in to show you sometime. At least Retha and Conrad, the oldest ones. They—"

"Well, ma'am, if you want to tell them what you do, what do you say, about where you work, and . . ."

"Oh, Fred, my grandbabies all know I'm their grand-mama. That's all I am and all I want to be."

"Yes ma'am, but . . . when I first came to Fenton's, I thought it might be an eating place—"

Dorothea snorts. "You mean like a restaurant proper?"

"Well, I know that's not right." I jerk my head up. You want to be careful not to say the wrong thing to Dorothea. She can turn on you, quick as anything. "Though I reckon there's not any place with food as good as we can get here."

"I reckon not," Dorothea says. She's dead serious.

"Well, my mama calls it a saloon, but—"

Dorothea folds her arms. Leans against the sink. "Fred," she says, "I been working for Mr. Fenton Calhoun for, I'd say, nigh onto eight years now." Shakes her head. "You know how boys carry on their foolishness, shooting marbles for keeps, hiding out in trees, fighting, swapping, making deals."

"Yes ma'am."

"Well, Mr. Fenton, he's a grown man, but he never gave up on any of that." Dorothea unfolds her arms and feels around her one pocket. Takes out a couple of crumpled dollar bills. Transfers them to her other pocket. "That's for my daughter," she says. "Her part."

I nod.

"Never wanted to give it up, as far as I can tell." She stands up straight. "So that's all this place is, a . . ." She waves her hands around. "What you boys call it?"

I shake my head. I don't know.

Dorothea snaps her fingers. "Clubhouse," she says. "That's it. Mr. Fenton's Fine Establishment's nothing but a big old clubhouse."

I laugh. She's right about that. I think back to this ramshackle place Mac Tower and Sid Jones set up on the creek. That's what Mac called it all right. His clubhouse.

"And as for my little bit of cooking, and Mr. Fenton's *convenience*"—Dorothea rolls her eyes up to the ceiling on Fenton's favorite word—"you know what that's all about, don't you?"

I shake my head.

"I'll tell you what breaks up a gang of grown men"—she raises her eyebrows—"or boys for that matter." She folds her arms. Nods at me. "Women." She winks. "And all that comes with them."

Women.

"So my ham biscuits and chili and whatnot"—she rolls her eyes again—"his *convenience* . . . That's all Mr. Fenton's way of keeping his gang together as long as he can." She looks at me. "You see?"

"Yes ma'am." I reckon.

"Keep them comfortable," she says. "Keep them coming." She laughs. Looks at the back door. "Lord," she says, "my babies going to be wondering what happened to me." Dorothea hustles out the door without even saying good-bye.

I slip on out the back door myself. If Fenton's forgot all about the barbecue, I'll just forget about it myself. I sure won't bother with cutting any wood today.

Fourteen

Two cars are parked in front of the house. A bicycle leans up against the front steps. The front hall's not dark like usual. Candles sit on the table under the picture rug. I've never seen that before. Lots of little candles, all burning at the same time. It's like walking into the middle of a dream.

The door to Susannah Doolittle's apartment is wide open. I move in a little closer. There's a big glass bowl filled up with red punch. A lot of people. I fix on this one girl with curly hair pulled up in a high ponytail. I think I've seen her come and go out of Susannah's a few times. She looks down the front of her white dress. Dabs with a napkin on her chest where she's spilled some of that punch. I don't reckon that'll ever come out.

Kenneth Lee pops up right in front of me. He has a cup of red punch in one hand. He grins fit to beat the band. Holds a plate up in my face. Sugar cookies and a piece of Mama's double-chocolate devil cake.

"Did Mama hold me back a piece?"

Kenneth Lee shakes his head. "Miss Susannah said for you to come on in and get yourself a plate."

I look over his shoulder. That girl's still going at that stain, but she's got a look on her face like she knows it's no use. Mama might could help her. She's good with stains. "Mama in there?"

Kenneth Lee shakes his head. "Come on," he says. "It'll all be gone."

I step back. "I've got to wash up."

"Can't," he says.

"I can't wash up?" I grab onto the railing. I'm too worn-out for this foolishness.

"That's what I said, Fred." Kenneth Lee giggles. He loves that little rhyme. "Mama waxed the front room. She locked the door, so it won't get tracked."

I let go of the railing. "So I'll go in the back." Seems like a strange time for Mama to be cleaning floors. I would have thought she'd want to come down here. Get in on the party.

Kenneth Lee shrugs. "Might miss out," he says. "Cake might be gone."

"You go get me a piece."

Susannah pops up behind him. "Come on in here, Freddy James." She reaches around and takes my arm. "Get yourself some refreshments."

"I got to wash up, ma'am."

"Well," she says. "Fix yourself a plate"—she points over in the corner—"and then you can go up by my stairs."

I nod. Something about her looks different.

"I thought you might like this, too." She gives me a book with a blue cover. Sets a glass saucer on top of it. "Help yourself."

"Thank you, ma'am." I look around. Kenneth Lee's sitting in a straight chair over by the door. Eating a cookie. Grinning. That girl with the red stain is gone. I bet she slipped out the door and went home in her ruined dress. Too bad. It had that stiff, just-bought look.

Susannah's leaning over, talking to a short little old lady. The one I saw in the drugstore. Miss Caroline, I think Roberta called her. I don't see Roberta.

Susannah looks up at me. Points. "Over there by the window."

"Yes ma'am." I look at her. It's her hair that's different. Higher. Harder.

There's only one man in here, far as I can see. Over by the food table. Wearing a brown jacket. You'd have to be plain crazy to wear a jacket in this heat.

Mama's cake is cut in pieces so thin that you can't rightly call them slices. More like slivers. That's how Minnie Tower used to eat her cake. "Just cut me a sliver," she'd say. Minnie, she'd always end up eating at least three or four slivers, but only one at a time.

I lay three of them on my plate, along with two cookies and two of those little triangle sandwiches. Dip myself out a cup of punch. Head on over to the back stairway. I never been in there before.

I close the door behind me, and everything goes black.

I move my cup onto the plate. Reach up and around for the chain. Find it and pull on the light. On the walls, all the way up to the top, are pictures. Most of them are photographs. One up toward the middle, though, looks like a painting.

I move on up to that one. Right before it there's a picture of Miss Precious, looking just like herself except that her hair's brown instead of white. I like the painted one. It's of that Eiffel Tower over in France. Down in the corner, written in red, is S. Doolittle. I reckon Susannah painted this picture herself. That's amazing.

Off to the side of that, in a fancy red frame, is a picture of Bucky Kent, all done up in uniform. That surprises me. The last picture is another big one of Miss Precious with her white hair, but stuck in the corner of the frame is a little faded photograph. It's of a young girl in a movie star pose. It might be Susannah Doolittle herself, when she was little, but I can't say for sure.

Susannah opens up the door at the bottom of the stairs. Reaches for the light cord. "You all the way up?"

"Yes ma'am."

"All right then." She turns off the light.

I set the book and plate and cup down on the table. Eat a sliver of cake. I've waited about as long as I'm able on that.

"Good?" Mama's slouched in the chair in the front room.

I nod.

"I waxed myself into a corner." Mama wouldn't have

done that without meaning to. She rubs her temples, like maybe she has a headache.

I eat another sliver of cake. Take a sip of that punch. "You didn't want to go downstairs?"

Mama shakes her head. Squeezes her eyes shut. "They're all dressed up down there."

I get up. There's a whole quart of milk, so I pour myself a glass. "That punch is awful," I say.

Mama laughs. "It's nice down there, isn't it?"

I shrug. "I reckon." Take a bite of sugar cookie. Straighten up that book. *Huckleberry Finn.*

"So full of nice"—Mama straightens up. Rolls her hands around—"*little* touches."

"Like what?" Susannah's apartment was nice enough, but I didn't see anything special about it.

Mama looks at me. Blinks. "Lace." That's what she comes up with. "A lot of little lace touches."

I reckon. It puts me in mind of an old lady's house. Close and full. Those pictures in the staircase were interesting, though. I nod my head over that way. "You ever been down those stairs?"

Mama shakes her head. "No."

"She's got a lot of pictures hanging in there." I lower my voice. "She's got one of Bucky Kent. I thought she hated him."

"Well," Mama says, "I reckon if you ever love somebody, and they love you, I reckon you can't ever really be rid of them, even if you want to." Mama leans back. Squeezes her eyes shut again.

I wonder what Mama would do if Daddy just walked up to our door one day. First off, I know there'd be a lot of yelling, but when that settled down, I just don't know. Would we stay here? Would we move away? Could we get the farm back? I don't know. "I think I'll go lay down for a while."

Mama nods.

"You could have worn your green dress," I say. "That's nice." Daddy thought that was Mama's prettiest dress. He always said that, when she was getting dressed for church or something special. "Wear that nice green one," he'd say.

"I'm tired of that green dress," Mama says. She doesn't open her eyes.

"Mama! Look, Mama!" Kenneth Lee yells.

My eyes pop open. I jump up off my pallet and run out into the kitchen. Kenneth Lee's arms are full of little zucchinis and tomatoes.

Mama's sitting at the table. She looks up. "Well, my Lord, will you look at that."

"Where'd you get all that?" I ask him. You'd think he's dug up a pot of gold, the way he's grinning and hopping back and forth.

"Why, it's from Kenneth Lee's very own garden." She smiles at him. "Right?"

Kenneth Lee nods up and down. Breathes hard. Me and Mama both, we can't help but laugh at him, but he doesn't get mad. I don't think he even notices. "There's some green beans, too." He grabs Mama's hand. "They might be too little, I don't know." He hops on one foot. "Come and see."

"Oh, all right." Mama slides her feet into her shoes.

I follow them down the back steps. I hadn't paid much attention to Kenneth Lee's little garden. Those scraggly tomato plants are bushy and chock full of yellow blossoms. Bean and zucchini vines climb on the railing.

I remember Daddy sitting Kenneth Lee up on the tractor seat. "I swear, boy," he said, "you got red dirt running in your veins instead of blood." He looked at me and laughed. "This boy's more a farmer than you or me could ever be." Daddy was right about that. I seen plenty of people with that special connection, that special comfort with the outdoors, just like Kenneth Lee. Hoyt Axel and Uncle Cecil and Aunt Crayton, they all had it, that way of picking up an ear of corn and seeing what had been and what was going to be, all in that ear of corn. I look at an ear of corn, and I just see something to go alongside beans.

You can tell Kenneth Lee's been working at this garden. We haven't had any rain for the past eight days, but his plants stand up straight and bushy and tall.

Mama kneels down. Fingers the green beans. "Give these another day or two, don't you think?"

Kenneth Lee nods. "Maybe tomorrow."

"Or the next day, maybe."

Susannah Doolittle stands out on her little porch and smokes a cigarette. "I like tomatoes." It's getting dark. I guess the tea's over.

Mama sits down on the second step. "Looks like there's plenty for everybody." I sit down on the one above her.

Kenneth Lee looks up at Mama. "I was going to take them around and sell them," he whispers to Mama.

"I think we'll be able to spare two or three," Mama whispers back.

"Everybody loved your cake, Eleanor."

"Really?"

Susannah laughs. "You know they did." She grinds out her cigarette in a dish on the railing. "Good-night all."

"Good-night," Mama says. She looks up. "I had an idea this afternoon." Grabs my arm. "I'm going to make five double-chocolate devil cakes."

"Five?"

"I'm going to cut them into slices, wrap them in wax paper, and sell them for ten cents apiece at that barbecue of yours." She frowns. "You think that's too much? You think a nickel's better?"

"Depends on the slice." I wouldn't give two cents for those tiny little pieces at Susannah's party.

"You think Fenton would mind?"

"If we get back home by August, we might be able to put in some fall crops. Maybe some cabbage and carrots." Kenneth Lee pulls on Mama's sleeve. "How long you reckon we going to stay here in town?"

Mama looks at me. We'd whispered about it a little, back and forth, about how we're going to tell Kenneth Lee the farm is gone. What's the difference? That's the way I see it. What's the rush? That's what Mama says. Let him hold on to the idea a little longer. No harm in that.

"It'll all work out," Mama says.

"I don't think Fenton would mind at all," I say. "I think Fenton would think it's a good idea." It is a good idea. "We're going to get the pig tomorrow."

"Well," Mama says, "I've got a *real* good idea." She straightens up and stretches her arms out and back. "Why don't we go up and make ourselves some tomato sandwiches."

Mama slices up the tomatoes. I get out the mayonnaise. Daddy was right. I'm not much on growing things. Taking care of the farm, that was just a job to me. Something I had to do. Something I didn't have any trouble leaving behind.

Still, nothing makes a place your home like eating food you just picked out of a garden right outside your door. I sprinkle on some pepper. Take a bite. "These are real good, Kenneth Lee," I say.

Up until just now, this apartment was just where I came to sleep and eat. I take another bite. Mama sets out some pickles and milk. It's funny that Kenneth Lee would be the one to make it something more. Seeing as how he's the only one who doesn't know this is all we've got.

Fifteen

Mitch and his boys are gone. We're back to the business of the barbecue. Today we get the pig.

Dorothea's coming along because she knows what's what when it comes to buying a pig. Evelyn's coming along because Fenton's giving her a ride out to her mama's to see her little girl. And I'm coming along because Fenton asked me if I wanted to, and I said yes.

Dorothea sits across from me in the back of Fenton's pickup. She pulls a pink ribbon into a bow to hold down her straw hat. "Mr. Fenton better get a move on," she says. "Before the sun gets too high."

Fenton comes out. Bangs on the hood. Flashes a big smile. "Ready to get us a pig?"

"I've been ready," Dorothea says.

"Sun's fierce, son," Fenton says. He sets a straw hat on my head. Laughs. Climbs in behind the wheel. Lays on the horn a couple of times.

Evelyn wobbles out the back door, climbs up front, in the cab, beside Fenton. I don't think much of Evelyn.

Everything about her is loud. Her hair. Her clothes. Her laugh. And I sure don't think much of anybody that leaves her little girl off with someone else to raise.

Dorothea straightens her hat. Pulls the brim down closer to her eyes. I reckon I roll my eyes too big and let on my feelings about Evelyn, because she points her finger at me. "You behave," she says. "That girl's had herself a hard time, and she does the best she can."

I shrug. Fenton cranks up the truck. I hold on to my hat. Settle back into the dust and noise. Dorothea closes her eyes. I can't hear her, but I can tell by the set of her mouth she's over there humming one of her hymns.

Once we turn onto 42, I get to thinking about the farm. Get to thinking about what it would have been like if we hadn't moved into town. If we'd just let one day slide into another until Miss Precious rolled up in her black Ford and told us, "You can't live here anymore."

Maybe Daddy wouldn't have let that happen. Maybe he has a plan, and I just can't see it. That Odysseus didn't get home after the Trojan War, for—what was it?—maybe ten, fifteen years. But, boy, once he got there, he took up that bow. Bent it. Shot through those axes. Showed all those troublemakers what's what. Maybe I ought to have a little more faith in Daddy, but it's not easy, what with the way everything's come about.

Fenton stops. Pulls up in front of what I reckon is Evelyn's mama's house. Maybe Evelyn's little girl doesn't have it so bad, living out here with her grandma and aunt and cousins. The house looks decent enough. I see cornstalks and bean rows out back. A fair amount of chickens peck around in the yard.

A girl, around Kenneth Lee's age, lazes on a swing on the porch. I wonder if that's her. I wonder if Evelyn has that same dirty blond hair under that orange mess on her head. Nobody's told me, but I figure that has to be a dye job. I look at that Roberta's red hair, and it's different—it's got a shine to it.

I can make out a woman standing behind the screen door, but neither one of them, not the little girl or the woman, makes a move to come out to Evelyn. Just look at her. Don't wave or anything.

Fenton gets out and goes around to open the door for Evelyn. She climbs out. Smiles. Waves. Bounces up and down like there's a crowd running for her, with wide-open arms, calling out her name. A boy, just a kid, like the girl, appears from out behind the house. He stares at us. The girl and the woman stay put.

Dorothea stirs. Opens her eyes. Watches Evelyn wobble across the dirt in her high heels. Shakes her head. It does make you feel a little sad for Evelyn. Seeing so much energy on one side, and just plain nothing on the other.

Fenton climbs back in. Roars down the dirt road. Dorothea closes her eyes. I turn my face out of the wind. Fenton turns off on the creek road. That's good. It wouldn't bother me, but I'd just as soon not have to ride by the farm.

At John Kaye's place, an old guy—who I figure to

be John Kaye—waves Fenton around back. Fenton parks off to the side of the pigpen, lets down the tailgate, and helps Dorothea down. I hop out over the side. Me and Fenton just stand back and let Dorothea look over the seven pigs. John Kaye first off moves along with her, but then he steps aside, too.

"She knows her swine, I reckon," John says to Fenton.

Fenton nods. "That she does."

I remember back when Daddy had to have a man come out to find the place to dig a new well. We couldn't take our eyes off him. He strutted around. Looked up at the sky. Rubbed his feet on the ground.

"What's he doing?" I asked Daddy.

Big Kenny laughed. "Putting on his show." Folded his arms. "Can't start digging too quick, Freddy James, else we might think he's not worth the money he's charging." Winked at me. "It's bad business to skip the show."

All those pigs look pretty much the same to me, but Dorothea takes her own sweet time. Squats down. Nods her head. Frowns. Moves on to the next one. Gives that same careful over and under look. I figure it's a show, and it's a mighty good one.

Finally she stands up. Points out the one over in the far corner. That's a nice touch. Me and Fenton and John Kaye muck on through the mud and pull that poor squealer out of his cool corner. "You want me to try and box him or—"

Fenton looks over at Dorothea. She shakes her head. "Just tie him."

Boxing would have been easier. Now we're our own kind of show, me and Fenton and John Kaye, trying to get a hold of the squirmy pig and hoist it up onto the truck. Dorothea just stands back and watches us. Keeps her arms folded. Doesn't crack a smile. Takes it serious. That's the best part of the Dorothea show. That serious expression on her face. It's hard for me not to laugh.

We finally get the pig tight enough to stay put, but loose enough to roll around. I feel in my pocket. Two quarters and four dimes. I sidle up to Dorothea. "How much you think he'd take for a chicken?"

Dorothea cocks her head. "A chicken?" Narrows her eyes. "A chicken?"

"Yes ma'am." I whisper, hoping it'll encourage her to lower her own voice. "I thought I might pick one up for Kenneth Lee—that's my brother." I shake my head. "You know, he had a chicken back on the farm—sort of a pet—and we had to leave it behind."

"No," Dorothea says. "A pig's one thing. I'm not riding back to town with any chicken." She pats my shoulder. Leans down close to my ear. "I'll do something for the boy." She gives Fenton her hand, and he helps her back up. She lifts her skirt and steps carefully around the pig that's already made itself at home.

"You want to sit up front?" Fenton asks me. "On the way over to pick up Evelyn?"

I shake my head. Climb on back into my corner across

from Dorothea. Fenton cranks up. I hold on to my hat. Try closing my eyes.

What I like about Dorothea is she never carries on, and she never says anything just to be nice. Or just to shut you up. She never hits you over the head with all the pleases and thank-yous and if you want me tos. She just says what she says and does what she does, without any folderol, so I'm not too surprised when she comes in the back door this morning with a chicken.

"You think this'll do for the boy?" She's holding up one of those parakeet birdcages, and it's all filled up with a hen. "It's a guinea, but that might be better, for here in town." She sets the cage on the floor and throws her pocketbook under the counter. "Take it home to him now." Ties on her apron. "We've got a lot to do today."

"Thank you, ma'am." Until just now, I'd forgotten all about the chicken business. "Kenneth Lee'll love this."

"Hope your Susannah Doolittle won't mind." She waves me out the door. "Hurry on now."

I hadn't thought of that. What Susannah Doolittle might think about a chicken pecking around in her yard. You don't see much of that on River Street. But even if she doesn't like it, I don't think Susannah'll have the heart to take it from Kenneth Lee once he has it. She might be put out with me, but so what?

Kenneth Lee's out in his garden. Looks like those beans are ready. He's filling up one bucket with them and another one with tomatoes.

"Hey," I say. "Look at this."

Kenneth Lee looks up. His mouth drops open. "Where'd you get that guinea?"

"Dorothea brought it in." I hold the cage out to him. "You want it?"

"Yeah." He takes the cage. Holds it out and looks at it. Breaks into a grin.

"I've got to give that cage back," I say. "So take it on out." Kenneth purses up his lips. Clucks at that creature. I laugh. No way Susannah'll make him get rid of it.

He sets down the cage. Gets down on his knees and unsnaps the door. "Come on," he says. "Come on, Toby."

I roll my eyes. Toby. No way I'll ever warm up to something with a beak. Not like that.

"How come?" he says.

"How come what?"

"How come the lady gave it to you?"

"She thought you might like it."

I thought it might take some time, but the guinea squeezes out into Kenneth Lee's hands. He's still clucking and whatnot. I reckon he speaks the language.

I pick up the cage. "See you tonight."

"Tell the lady—"

"Dorothea."

Kenneth Lee nods. "Tell her I said thank you."

"Yeah," I say. "I will." I run up the back steps. I need a drink of water.

Mama's ironing. Two stacks of laundry are already bundled up on the table. There's a whole other load drying on the line outside. She frowns. "What's that."

"Birdcage." I pour myself a glass of water. "I've got to get it back to Dorothea."

She wrinkles up her nose. Nods.

I finish off the water. Set the glass on the counter. "I got to get back."

"Did you mention about selling the cake to Fenton."

I shake my head. "Not yet, but I will. It's fine."

Mama upends her iron. "Sit down just for a minute."

"I got to—"

"Just for a minute." Mama sits down. Pats the table with her hand. "Fenton's not going anywhere."

"Okay." I sit down across from her. Lean in on my elbows. What now?

"I've been getting together Kenneth Lee's papers for registering him at the school in the fall, and Susannah said I might have to get him a checkup over at the health department." She shrugs. "I reckon that might just be a good idea anyway." She clears her throat. "And I thought it might be a good idea for you to get one, too."

"I feel fine."

"For school."

"I'm not going to school, Mama. I got a job."

"Well . . ." She straightens up. Taps her fingers on the table. "Susannah . . . and Miss Precious, too—she mentioned it particular when I went over there—seem to think that you ought to be signing up for school."

"Well, I don't see as how it's any of their concern." I stand up. "I'll look into it, but"—I shrug—"I got a job."

"Well, Miss Precious, she seemed to think—"

"I don't care what Miss Precious thinks." I might have looked into this school if she hadn't brought Miss Precious into it. I'm tired of hearing about what Miss Precious thinks. What she thinks people ought to do. What she might do if they don't. "I got my own plans."

"Plans?" Mama makes it sound like something wicked.

"I might like to go into business for myself." I shake my head. "I'm learning a lot about that over at Fenton's."

"I can imagine," Mama says. "So you want yourself a saloon like Fenton."

"No ma'am." I shake my head. I don't know as I'd want to be in charge of all the ruckus that goes on at Fenton's. Paulie tells me there's at least two or three fights in the bar every night. "I'd like more just a regular store." I haven't altogether thought it through. I guess I ought to.

Mama breaks into a big smile. "You know," she says. "I've always wanted to own a business myself." She looks out the window over the sink. Nods her head. "A dress shop, maybe."

"You'd be a heap better at it than that snooty Hennie Crenshaw."

"You think so?" She sits up straight. Bounces a little

in her chair. You'd think she was talking to Minnie Tower.

"Yes ma'am." I take a couple of steps toward the door.

"Maybe we could go in together. Really do it. Kenneth Lee could help out."

"Well." I got my hand on the screen door. "I don't see myself selling dresses."

Mama waves the dresses away. "Any kind of store." She shrugs. "A diner."

A diner. I laugh. "I bet we could do it." I bet we could.

"But even so," Mama says, "don't you think you might do both?" She raises her eyebrows. "Go to school and . . . the other."

"Maybe." My hand drops off the door handle. "But don't you think I might learn more about running a business working over at Fenton's than I would sitting in some school?"

Mama nods. She can't help but see the sense of it. "Maybe."

I open the door. "I got to go."

"Freddy James—?"

"Ma'am?" I don't have time for all this talking.

"We'll talk about it some more, but I know whatever you set your mind to do, you'll do a fine job of it."

That's about the nicest thing Mama's ever said to me. I feel like I want to hug her, but I don't have the time. I nod, wave, and let the door slam behind me.

It wasn't just what Mama said; it was the way she'd looked at me, too. I'd seen that look one time before. Back when I was still in school, I asked Miss Keitel if she had any more books about the Trojan War or Odysseus or any of those other Greek fellows. I almost didn't ask—thought I might be putting her to some trouble—but she just seemed as happy as could be. Better than happy. Delighted would be the word. "Freddy James, you just made my day," she said. "You can just be sure I'll find you some more books on those Greeks."

Of course, she didn't. It wasn't more than two weeks later that she married that soldier and was gone, but that didn't take away much from the way that look made me feel. Like I was smart. Like I might go someplace. Like I might do something more than just get by.

Sixteen

Dorothea's got me peeling potatoes, boiling potatoes, and cutting potatoes into little cubes. I spend the better part of the day on potato salad. When I get that done, I start two pots of pinto beans soaking. Dorothea's going to put the beans on to bake tomorrow; we both have to be in before five in the morning.

When I've done all I can do today, I head on back to Fenton's office. Take him a glass of his medicine, just in case. He drinks it down.

"Fenton," I say. "My mama's going to be selling slices of her double-chocolate devil cake at the barbecue." It's been a long day. No need to get into a discussion about it. Best to just tell him straight out, like it's a known fact.

Fenton sighs. Closes his eyes. Nods.

Mitch and his boys are back. I expected them to show up driving down the street in a parade of cars, but Mitch just rolls in driving a plain old black pickup. The other three, including Sam Davis, are all piled up in the back.

"Where's the cars?"

"They left them out at the Lawrence boy's place," Dorothea says. "To get fixed up."

It's not easy, but I find a clean spot on the counter to write up a sign with Fenton's India ink. "Eleanor's Double-Chocolate Devil Cake—5 Cents." Then I grab an empty liquor box and cut out for home. Dorothea's already gone.

Yesterday Susannah brought home a ham for Mama to cook and split with her, like we did before with the chicken. We had enough left over for supper tonight, and probably tomorrow night, too. When we finish eating, the five double-chocolate devil cakes are cooled and ready to slice. Mama sets aside a slice for us to split when we're finished. We all promise to not even eat a crumb until we're done wrapping, because we might get carried away. Mama's got squares of wax paper torn and stacked on the table, ready to go.

"I think we ought to get a dime for these," Kenneth Lee says.

"They're worth ten cents," I say, "but I think she'll sell more for a nickel."

Mama nods.

"And I could squeeze you in a place on the table—Dorothea said we could—but—"

"You don't think Fenton—?"

"No," I say. "He's fine with it, I'm just wondering . . ." I wrap faster than either one of them. I want to get done. "If your cake's on the table, people might think it's included in the seventy-five cents for the barbecue plate—"

"We got the sign!" Kenneth Lee says.

"Yeah, but you see, you start off on the wrong foot with people, if you right from the start have to tell them the cake's extra, that it'll cost them a nickel more." Kenneth Lee blinks. He doesn't get it. I look at Mama. "You know how people are. Always afraid they're being tricked. . . ."

Mama nods.

"You want them to feel good about the cake." I tuck and fold the wax paper on the last piece. "Like it's their idea."

Mama lights up. "That is so true." She points at me. "Your brother's going to be a rich man someday, Kenneth Lee."

Kenneth Lee blinks. We might as well be talking Susannah Doolittle's French to him, for all he understands.

I point to the empty box. "I thought we ought to cut out the front, like a display case, so folks could reach right in."

Mama nods. "That's a good idea." She turns the box over. "I think it's too wide to fit on the wagon, though."

"I can carry it over for you in the morning."

"How come we don't just put the cake right in the wagon and pull it over," Kenneth Lee says.

I shake my head. "It's too banged up."

"We could cover it up," he says. "With the quilt."

Me and Mama, we both look at him. "That's a good

idea," Mama says. "Except I think we ought to use the red-checked tablecloth."

I nod. "That does make more sense." I got a lot to do in the morning. I don't need to be keeping up with a box of cake on top of it all.

Kenneth Lee grins. "I reckon I'm going to be a rich man, too."

Mama laughs. "Well," she says, "whoever gets rich, just remember"—she winks at me—"all for one, and—"

"One for all," Kenneth Lee says.

I smile. "Well, I got to get to bed." Breathe in all that heavy chocolate smell. Dream of eating double-chocolate devil cake all night long.

Everybody comes. About eleven-fifteen, Mama and Kenneth Lee pull in with their wagon load of cake. They park over to the side of the long serving table.

Mama's wearing a dress I've never seen before. Long and full. Big purple flowers on yellow.

"This the chicken boy?" Dorothea asks.

"Yes ma'am," I say. "This is my brother, Kenneth Lee, and this is my mama, Eleanor." I never have seen a dress look so pretty—not on anybody—as that one does on my mama. I bet if Daddy could see her right now, he'd be sorry he ran off.

"Thank you for the guinea, ma'am," Kenneth Lee says. "I named him Toby."

Dorothea laughs. "I reckon one that'll name poultry sure needs to have some poultry around." She leans down and breathes in the chocolate. "I'm going to have me a piece of this."

Mama smiles. "Thank you." She nods her head down at Kenneth Lee. "For . . . you know."

Dorothea nods. Winks at Kenneth Lee. Hurries on back to the pit.

"Where'd you get that dress?" I ask Mama.

She leans down. "I worked out a little something with Miss Hennie. Sort of a layaway"—she bobs her head back and forth—"worked out with the laundry."

"It's real pretty," I say, and run on after Dorothea. "What do you want me to do?"

"Roll up the wire on that end," Dorothea says. "I want to pour on some more sauce."

"Fenton said it was all right," I say. "To just leave it be."

"Uh-huh," Dorothea says. "I heard him."

I lift up the corner rocks and roll back the wire. Dorothea pours on a panful of sauce and brushes it over the pig with what I reckon is a broom.

"You did good." I look around, up over my shoulder, and there stands Jacob.

"Hey, you think so?" Jacob's shirt's bright white. His pants a silky black. Loose in the front. Different from anything I've ever seen, but sharp enough to be some kind of uniform. "You wear that on your railroad job?"

Jacob laughs. Jams his hands deep in his pockets. The pants go even wider. Really different. "No man," he says. "These are my party clothes."

He shakes his head. Reaches up and wipes the sweat back into his hair. "How's it doing."

Dorothea stands up. "Good," she says. I straighten out the wire and put the stones back down. "You go bring out those tubs of potato salad."

I run off into the kitchen. Jacob struts around. Waves here and there. He looks fine. Too fine for Fenton's. Too fine for Elderton. I like those pants.

I set the potato salad down on the long table, next to the metal tray Dorothea's got ready for the barbecue. It's empty, but Fenton, Dorothea, and Jacob are working over at the pit. Paulie's just standing back and watching.

Dorothea looks up. Calls out to me. "Cut up that cornbread and bring it on out."

There's a crowd gathering now. The women and children, they sure took it to heart and showed up. They sit out on the grass in back. Stand around the parking lot. Spill out into the streets. I never seen so many people in one place.

Dorothea doesn't have to tell me about the rest. The plates. The napkins. The knives and forks. The beans. The butter Dorothea had me cut into little patties. I just go ahead and set it all up on the table.

Fenton's head stands up over most of the folks. He's looking down. At the pit. He's always worrying over something. I run in and fix up a glass of his medicine.

He takes it. Sighs. Closes his eyes. Drinks it down. Opens his eyes. "You tasted it yet?"

I shake my head.

"Well, get over there behind the table with Dorothea and Paulie." He winks. "There's plenty." Waves me on. "You'll get yours."

Dorothea's behind the meat platter. That figures. She's not going to trust that to us. She pushes Paulie behind the potato salad. Points me to the beans and cornbread. The folks are lined up and ready to move. After about the first ten plates or so, I get a rhythm going and stop dripping beans on the table. Square of cornbread. Pat of butter. "Happy Fourth," I say. "Enjoy yourself." Same as Dorothea.

Four pickers and singers set up over in the corner under the trees. After about another five plates, I get a new rhythm going with their music. They change into one of those slow songs Mama likes. I give up on that. Block them out. Beans. Bread. Butter. "Happy Fourth."

Once I remember to glance over at Mama and Kenneth Lee. The stack of cake is down past the top of the wagon. Fenton did think to put out some packaged fried pies, but as far as I can tell, most folks are coming up with a nickel for Mama's cake. She could have baked another two or three of them.

I catch that picture of our own place of business again. Mama up behind the counter smiling. Kenneth Lee pumping some gas. No matter what kind of business we have, I figure to have a gas pump. Fenton's talking about putting one out front himself. Just makes good sense. And I see me back in an office counting up money and paying some boy his weekly wage.

The first line slows down. Thins out. Then a second one forms. Starts up again. Jacob brings over another big tray of meat. Fenton strolls by. Raises his eyebrows at Dorothea. Nods his head. I bet he hasn't eaten one bite. Dorothea says that if Fenton would just eat regular, his stomach wouldn't give him so much trouble. Fenton says he can't eat when he's working. "And I'm always working," he says.

Dorothea laughs whenever she hears that. "Is that what you call it?"

Mr. Cooper from the drugstore holds out his plate. Leans over the bean pot. "Those look delicious." He gives me a big smile.

"Yes sir." I spoon them onto his plate. Bread and butter him. He pushes that smile on everybody. Not really looking straight at any one person. Just smiling all around, so that it doesn't mean anything. I hate that.

He puts his arm around the short, curly-haired lady with him. Pushes her forward. "Move it along, dear." His wife, I reckon. His tone's not particularly nice, but he keeps that smile.

"Miss Precious!" Thank goodness Dorothea yells out. I'm so into my rhythm, I'd have probably spooned beans right into Miss Precious's bare hands. Nobody should get into a food line without a plate.

"Dorothea." Miss Precious takes her hand. Pulls her closer. "Everybody that goes up to Fenton carrying on about how good the food is, I'm sending them over to you," she says. "I know whose show this is."

"You go on, Miss Precious." Dorothea's smiling a bigger smile than I've ever seen her smile. "Get out of this line. I'll fix you up a plate myself." She runs around the table. Brings the line to a stone cold stop.

Mrs. Cooper clogs it up even worse. "Miss Precious?" She pushes back to the beans area. "Miss Precious?"

Miss Precious steps out of the line. Mrs. Cooper steps out with her. "Miss Precious," Mrs. Cooper says. "I just want to thank you again for that generous contribution to the missionary fund."

Dorothea pushes on through fixing Miss Precious's plate. I take on double duty. Meat and beans. Paulie picks up on the cornbread.

Mr. Cooper's red-headed niece Roberta comes up next. Rolls her eyes. Leans in close to me. "Can I get two pieces of cornbread. I don't want any beans."

I nod. Make it quick. Dorothea's been firm on that point. No special orders. "Don't be too friendly," she said. "Just friendly enough." Dorothea's worked a lot of food lines. "Keep it moving. That's all you got to do." At least that was the rule until Miss Precious cut into line.

"I guess you didn't learn your job as good as I thought." Jacob's hand is on my shoulder.

"She didn't want beans," I say.

"Haven't you learned to take a break now and again?" He pushes me back. Steps up behind the beans. "Go on," he says. "Get yourself something to eat."

I appreciate it all right, but truth is, I guess I'm a lot

like Fenton. No matter how good it smells, eating's something I'd rather do at the end of the day, when all the action's over. I sure don't feel like eating a regular meal in the middle of a crowd. Mama's got a few slices of cake left. "Can I have one?"

Mama smiles. "Sure you can." Nods at a lady standing beside her. "This is my other son," she says. "Freddy James."

The lady touches Mama's arm. "We'll be looking for you at church on Sunday." Rushes off after her own little kid.

Mama nods at me. "Central Baptist," she whispers. Only last week she'd said that as soon she got a proper invitation, she'd start back up going to church regular. "Nothing worse than marching into a new church without a proper invitation," she said. "They'll stare." Shook her head. "Burn a hole right through you."

I take a piece of cake.

"I had one already," Kenneth Lee announces.

I spot that Roberta sitting over by herself on a riser and stroll over.

"Hey." I sit down beside her and unwrap my cake. "Good?"

She nods. Swallows. "You cook it?"

I shake my head. Nod over at Dorothea back dishing out barbecue. Smiling at all the compliments. "Dorothea's the cook," I say.

"My Aunt Maggie, it's not that her cooking's bad . . ." Roberta's eyes narrow. She lays the cornbread down on her plate. Looks around until she sees the Coopers at a safe distance. "It just doesn't taste like . . . anything." She looks at me. "I miss my mama's cooking."

I take a bite of Mama's cake. It tastes like Christmas and every other good day I've ever had in my life.

Mr. Cooper laughs. It's a laugh that grates on your nerves. Ends up like he's out of breath. Gasping to get it back. Almost scary. Roberta and me both look up.

"How's he your uncle now?"

"By marriage." Roberta looks at me like I ought to know that. Like I've insulted her just asking. "Aunt Maggie, she's my mama's big sister."

"So you're just visiting?"

"It's my mama's idea. To keep me out of trouble while school's out." Roberta sets her plate down on the ground. "And, you know, maybe make a little money."

"He pay pretty good?"

Roberta shrugs. "I reckon, but he takes out for room and board." She unwraps her cake. "And he's so nosy." She shudders. "Always asking me where I'm going, what I'm doing." Rolls her eyes. "Says he wants to be able to give my mama a good report."

"What kind of trouble did you get in anyway?"

She slings back that red hair. "Oh, Mama just didn't like my boyfriend." She takes a bite of the cake. Nods. "This is good." She wipes her mouth. "Not that I like Simon so much anymore myself. He's only written me the one letter since I've been here, and it was kind of stupid."

I nod. Folks crowd around Mama's wagon. I reckon I'll only get the one piece.

"And then Mama and Daddy caught me sneaking out of the house one night, and just had a fit." She closes her eyes. Shakes her head. "They jerked me out of school two weeks early and sent me on into Elderton, they were so upset."

"You like it here?"

She shrugs. "I don't like *him*, with all his high-and-mighty talk about what's right and what's wrong." Nods. "But yeah, I like working the fountain. And being in town." She scrunches up her nose. "We live out in the sticks."

I open my mouth to say I don't like Mr. Cooper much either, but decide I'd best keep it shut. No matter what she says, Mr. Cooper's part of her family. I see Kenneth Lee over there sitting in the wagon. I guess they sold out. "You got any brothers? Or sisters?"

Roberta holds up four fingers. Takes up another bite of cake.

"That's my brother." I point over at Kenneth Lee. "You know him?"

Roberta looks up. Follows my finger over to Kenneth Lee. Shrugs. "I don't know," she says. "Maybe."

So if Kenneth Lee did do something, it couldn't have been much. I reckon you'd remember a thief. The pickers start up the music again. A chubby lady with Minnie Tower style, blond sugar-water hair, hitches up her skirt and dances. That's all it takes to get the crowd into it.

Roberta laughs. I point out old Miss Caroline, jigging by herself on the far side.

And then I see him. That no-good, pasty-faced Custis Fullbright wearing that same big phony smile. I stuff the wax paper into my pocket. Dancers get in my way. I shove through. I can't spot Custis now. And I don't see Mama.

Dorothea clangs on the metal pan with a spoon. "Fred!"

I look down the street.

"Break's over." Dorothea waves me over. "Come on."

Seventeen

We've run out of beans, so Fenton knocks a dime off the price. Paulie goes on in to work the bar, so it's just me and Dorothea serving.

"What's got you so distracted?" Dorothea says.

"I just wonder where my mama's gone off to."

Dorothea spoons up some barbecue. Slaps it on the fellow's plate. I give him a little extra potato salad, to make up for the beans. We're almost out of cornbread, too.

Dorothea points down the street. "I saw her walking down that way. Talking to a gentleman." She snaps her fingers. "I never did get a piece of that cake." Points at me. "But I heard good reports on it."

The music's still playing, but after a while the line slows down to nothing. Fenton strolls up. Taps his fingers on the table. "It went good, don't you think?"

"Well, of course it did, Mr. Fenton." Dorothea looks at me. Shakes her head. Smiles. "How'd you expect it to go?"

"Good." Fenton looks at me. "Once the music stops," he says, "go ahead and tear down these tables."

We attend to a few more scragglers. Dorothea sends me inside for another jar of tea.

Roberta's waiting at the table when I come outside. Arms folded. Eyes narrowed. "Hasn't anybody," she says, "ever taught you how to just say a normal good-bye before you're on your way." She looks at Dorothea. Holds up two fingers. "Two times," she says, "I've been having what seems like a regular conversation with this boy, when he just jumps up and runs away like he's seen a ghost." Widens her eyes at Dorothea. "That sound normal to you?"

Dorothea laughs. Looks at me. "It doesn't sound right," she says.

I'm not interested in their foolishness now. "I had to catch my mama."

Roberta shrugs. "I just thought you ought to know." She swings that red hair around. "It leaves an impression like you're pure crazy." Looks at Dorothea. "That was real good barbecue, ma'am." Turns and walks away.

"So that your girlfriend?" Dorothea scrapes off the sides, into a pile in the middle.

"That's the girl that works over in the drugstore." There's no need for Dorothea to make comments like that.

Dorothea looks up. Catches Jacob's eye. Snaps her fingers. Nods him over. "I reckon," she says, "a girl could handle both those jobs." She hands the meat tray over to Jacob. "There's not enough here to make out a decent plate," she says. "Let's break these tables down."

It's after dark by the time I finally get home, but Mama and Kenneth Lee aren't there. I knock on Susannah's door. No answer.

I sit out on the front steps. Look up the street. Down the street. Slap at the mosquitoes. Get a picture all of a sudden of Custis Fullbright standing in front of me. Smirking. "What you doing, boy, out here all by your lonesome?" I can hear him say that. "Waiting for your mama?" Making fun of me.

I get up. Go on inside. Drink a glass of water. Look out the window. Look at that book Susannah Doolittle gave me to read. *Huckleberry Finn.* Run down that first page. It's filled up with words like "hain't" and "betwixt." Words you wouldn't find in Miss Keitel's literature. And Huckleberry Finn? What kind of name is that? I put the book down.

Kenneth Lee's wagon rattles into the backyard. I stare at the screen door. Mama swings on through. "Hey there," she says. She's all bright-eyed and bubbly. You'd think she'd just come off an afternoon with Minnie Tower and her movie magazines.

"How come you didn't tell me you were leaving?" I'm mad. I let her see it. "And where've you been all this time?"

"Out walking." Mama rubs her mouth with her finger.

"Walking where?"

Mama shrugs. "Down Main Street."

Kenneth Lee unties his bag of marbles. "We went down by the railroad tracks." Pours them on the floor.

"I saw him," I say. "I saw Custis Fullbright."

Mama nods. "That was Custis all right."

"He's going to take us down to Charleston," Kenneth Lee says.

Mama shakes her head at him.

"What?" I say.

"Charleston." Kenneth Lee thumps a marble into the wall. "Custis Fullbright's going to take us down to visit Grandma and Grandpa."

Mama leans in a little closer to me. "What you don't know, Freddy James, is that before Custis up and left, he asked me to marry him."

"You're already married." I can't believe she even says such a thing.

"To Daddy," Kenneth Lee says. He looks at me. "Right?"

"I know that." Mama's mouth narrows into a straight line. She's sure lost that bubbly look. "It just struck me as strange that right before running off like that, he came out with some crazy 'Will you marry me?' instead of just saying a simple good-bye." Sighs. "I just had a thing or two to say to him on that count."

Kenneth Lee grins. "She wasn't nice." Shakes his head. "Not nice at all."

"It's just a ride, Freddy James." Mama holds out her hand to me. "So we can finally get down to visit my family."

"Not me." I don't look at her. "I don't like Custis Fullbright."

Mama pulls her hand away. "Oh, I don't like him all that much either, but truth is, he feels bad about the way he acted." She smooths out the skirt of her new dress. "It's not like he'd be doing us a special favor, driving us down there. He's got himself a salesman job that's taking him to Charleston anyway."

"We can go to Grandpa and Grandma's on a bus. I . . ." Suddenly I wish I hadn't been holding back. I wish I'd told her about that money Miss Precious gave me. "I can get the money for the bus. I can get it tomorrow."

Mama turns up her nose. "The bus." Waves away that idea. "We can't show up down home on the bus. Do you know how pitiful that would look?" She shakes her head. "I can just hear my mama."

"Well, I'll get down to see Grandma and Grandpa Sullivan in my own way." I wave *her* away. "I'm not going anywhere with Custis Fullbright."

"Well, that's fine for you, Freddy James." Her lips draw up into a tight little knot. "I have to take my opportunities when they come along."

"What's so good about going with Custis Fullbright?"

"Listen, your daddy's gone, and I think it'll look better if I don't show up . . . all alone." She taps her fingers together. "He's got a nice car." Shrugs. "It'll just look better."

"So what?" I don't get it.

She sighs. "My mama takes a real dim view of women that travel on the bus."

"How come?" Kenneth Lee pipes up.

"Yeah." I nod at him.

"I don't know how come," Mama says. "I just know, and that's the end of it."

"Well," I say, "what if you get down there, and Custis doesn't want to bring you back."

Mama shrugs. "Well," she says, "if I have to take a bus back home, I will. That would be a completely new circumstance."

I don't get it, but she doesn't seem to much care. "I'm going to bed." I've been up since before five o'clock this morning.

"Well." Mama claps her hands. "Custis is coming over for supper tomorrow. We'll get it all worked out then."

"Good-night." I'll be sure not to be here. I stop. "You sell all the cake?"

"Every last piece," Mama says.

"Well," I say. "That's good." I reckon he should, but even Custis Fullbright can't keep me awake tonight. It's been a long day.

Some things I just do automatic every day. Stock the bar and the shelves. Wash up Dorothea's dishes and Paulie's glasses. Sweep out the pool room. Still, every morning I hunt down Fenton first thing and find out what the first order of the day is. That's what he always says, "Now, Fred, the first order of the day is . . . ," and, whatever foolishness it is, I do it.

This morning, though, I got to think me and Fenton'll see eye to eye on the "first order of the day." The whole parking lot, the storefront, clear down to the street is a downright disgrace. Those trash barrels me and Paulie set out, they're stuffed full enough, but it's hard to believe, seeing all that trash left behind on the ground. Offhand, I'd have to say women and children kick up a worse mess than the usual drunks and gamblers.

First, though, I go back to Jacob's old room. I figure he might have slept there last night. The door's open, but I knock anyway.

Jacob looks up. "You did a fine job, Fred." He closes up his bag. "I just came up to make sure you didn't disappoint me."

I go on in and sit on the bed. "You leaving?"

"Yes sir." He looks in the mirror. Pats his hair. It puts me in mind of that morning with Bucky Kent. "I got to get back to work."

"You like your railroad job then?"

He looks at me. "The railroad's not a job, Fred. It's a way of life." He looks at his watch. "My granddaddy worked on the train, but my daddy"—he chuckles—"he got off track." He opens his hands out. "Don't know how he ended up in this nowhere town." He winks at me. "No offense."

"Didn't you ask him?"

Jacob shrugs. "Some trouble." He picks up his bag. "I got to wait outside." Walks out into the hall.

I follow him. "Did you like living in that room?"

"Not particularly." We pass Fenton's office. He's at his desk. Jacob salutes him. Fenton winks. "Didn't particularly not like it either," Jacob says. "It was a room."

"I might move in there myself."

Jacob steps out the back door. "If I were you," he says, "I'd just stay put." He shades his eyes. Looks around. "You got a mess to clean up out here."

"That's the truth."

"There's a pick back in the storage shed." He thrusts his fist down and up. "Just stab the paper up into the can." Rubs his back. "Save some wear and tear." A truck pulls up beside us. Jacob waves. He opens the truck door.

"Let's go, buddy." The guy behind the wheel snaps his fingers.

Jacob puts his bag in back. Turns around and points his finger at me. Winks. Hops in and closes the door. They drive away. I go on into the shed to find that pick tool.

That keeps me busy all morning. Dorothea only works a half day, but she sets me out a gallon jug of water and a couple of cheese sandwiches. "Take some shade breaks, Fred," she says. "I seen some people break right down and die from heatstroke."

Last thing is to sweep the gravel back off to the side.

Fenton's a stickler for having his gravel in place. At first I just figure the crowd kicked the gravel around, but now I see it's all arranged in pictures, like faces, with gravel for eyes and noses and mouths. And there's a house with a chimney, with three little stones coming out like smoke. Kids. Always got to be into something.

It's almost two o'clock when Mitch drives up in a blue Chevrolet sedan. Usually he screeches in here, churning up the dirt and gravel, but today he parks the car, just as careful and even as can be, up under the oak tree.

Fenton comes out the back door. "How's it feel?"

Mitch shrugs. "Pulls to the right. I don't think you'd notice unless you were looking for it."

Fenton nods. Walks around the car. Leans down by the left front fender. Rubs it. "I can feel the bondo here."

"Yeah," Mitch says, "but like I said, you're looking for it."

Fenton steps back. Looks up and down that side. "What'd it look like before?"

Mitch grins. "It's a miracle." Pulls on his scraggly new beard. "A stone miracle."

Fenton rubs his hands together. "Okay, pull it around back." He looks at me. "I want you to wax it and buff it."

"Yes sir."

"Chrome. Tires. Everything. Like new."

"Yes sir." That's my afternoon. Waxing and detailing that car. There's nothing in Jacob's toolshed for cutting down the wear and tear on my arms and shoulders. When I'm done with that, I scrounge up some of Dorothea's biscuits and some milk. Go on back to Jacob's room and lie down.

Of course, waxing a car's nothing beside cutting wood. I been this tired before. But before I didn't have to worry about going home and finding Custis Fullbright there.

A yell from out front wakes me up. I don't know what time it is, but I figure it's safe to head on home.

Eighteen

Mama folds her blue skirt. Lays it into a little brown suitcase. I didn't know they'd be leaving so soon.

"Where'd you get that suitcase?" It looks to be real leather.

"Susannah's letting me borrow it." She looks over at Kenneth Lee. "Hand me those socks." Kenneth Lee gives them to her. She tucks them in a corner, under the skirt. Looks at me. "Your Grandma and Grandpa, they're going to be so disappointed."

Kenneth Lee takes off. Slams out the screen door. Probably checking up on his garden again. I reach down into my pocket. "Mama?"

"What?"

I pull a ten-dollar bill and ten ones out of my pocket. "I got some money. You don't need Custis. We can all go down together on the bus." I hold out the money to her.

She takes the money. Sits down on the bed. "Where did you get this?"

"I've been working really hard," I say.

"It doesn't matter." She lays the money on the bed. "We can't be showing up down there on a bus, like a bunch of sad sacks." She hops back up. Looks around the room. Takes that new yellow dress down from where it's hanging on the closet door. "Always save your best things for last," she says. "Put them on top." Lays it on the bed. Folds it up carefully, to just the size of the suitcase. "I'll have Custis stop so I can change into it before we get there."

"What's wrong with the bus?" I thought it all through last night. Figured if I let her know we had *some* money, she wouldn't need to go through with this. And here she acts like twenty dollars is nothing. Like it doesn't even matter. "If you go on down with Custis, it's your fault I'm not going."

"No." She shakes her head. "If you're too stubborn to go, it's your fault, Freddy James. Not mine." She closes the suitcase. "I don't expect you to understand, and I'm not trying to say anything bad about my family—I love them all—but I will not give them the satisfaction of showing up all poor and pitiful on a bus." She sits down on the bed. Squeezes her eyes like she's holding back tears. "I got this beautiful new dress." She waves her hand over the suitcase. "But, you know, it won't stay new forever." She sniffs. She is crying. "Custis looks good enough. He's got a car." She reaches for my hand. "He's already heading that way."

I go ahead and take her hand. It's just hanging there. Sit down beside her.

"It'll make a good impression, don't you see." She lets out a long breath. "Something for them to see before I start . . . explaining all that's happened."

"Yes ma'am." For the first time, I think maybe I do understand. It's just like Dorothea and the pig. The well man and his slow, careful carrying on with the stick. The new dress, Custis and his car, Susannah's leather suitcase, that's all just part of Mama's show. I can see the sense in that. She wants to tell them the truth, but you don't ever want anybody feeling sorry for you.

"If you don't want to ride with Custis, then maybe you could come down on the bus by yourself." Mama sniffs and smiles. "Then we could all come back together on the bus." Nods her head. "That would be all right."

I nod back at her. "In a few days maybe," I say, "after I work out something with Fenton."

She presses the twenty dollars into my hand. "So you hold on to this."

I shake my head. "You hold on to it so you can give Custis money for gas." That way I don't have to feel bad about it at all. It's a business arrangement. That's all. "I can come up with bus fare." Maybe I will go. "Right now, I've got to get to work." I jump up.

Mama pulls up, too, and hugs me. "Be good now," she says.

I hug her back. That's the first time that's happened in I don't know when, but I reckon more than likely it's my fault. "Yes ma'am," I say. "I will."

Fenton points me out the back door. "The Lawrence kid finished up all of them but one." There's five more cars parked out back. "Probably won't get that over here until tomorrow."

I hope not. There's my day. Washing and waxing. "They look good."

Fenton walks around the green Ford. "You think so?" He kneels down. Rubs a spot on the fender.

"Yes sir," I say. "I'd buy one."

"Well, that's fine." He stands up. "I wouldn't stop you." He rubs his finger along the window seal. "Except maybe for that blue one. Watch out for that, when they pull one way or the other like that. Usually means it's been wrecked." He squints at the hood of the black car like he sees something. "They'll try to tell you it's just the tires, but likely as not, it's chassis damage." He taps the door a couple of times.

I think about it for a few minutes. Would it be best to go a car at a time? Wash it, then wax it. Or would it be better to set up and wash all the cars, one after another, before I get on with the waxing? That sounds smarter.

The washing I don't mind. The thermometer moves past ninety before noon, and I don't worry about getting wet. It's more fun than work on a day like today.

Waxing, though, that's something else. Worse on the shoulders than cutting wood. I swear it is. I have to change to my left arm every once in a while, just to give my right one a rest. Can't do that for long, though. Just can't get the right rhythm going. If I can see streaks up close, I reckon old eagle-eye Fenton could see them standing down on the street corner. At first, I can't see any of what Fenton sees, but after a while some of the rough spots, dings, and dents jump out at me.

Around four I start hearing rumbles. I half worry about a storm popping up right now and ruining my wax jobs, and I'm half praying for one, just to put an end to this day right now. That's how tired I am. That's how hot it is. It's more than the heat. The air's got that dead, dirty feeling that just weighs you down. I swear, it's giving me a sore throat.

I get done, though, without any rain. It's just as well. Good as it would have felt, I'd regret it in the morning, having to start that work all over again.

Fenton inspects them. Up close and at a distance. "Look good," he says. "Go on in and check the bar."

I put out clean glasses for Paulie and stock the bar. When it's finally time to go home, it hits me I got nothing to go home to. I take a bowl of pork rinds out of the bar. Go back into Jacob's room and lay down.

"What are you talking about?"

I sit up. Some commotion in the hall. I was afraid of that. Evelyn coming crashing in here with one of her boyfriends.

"The boy's been here since daybreak. Just because his mother is—"

I swing my feet around onto the floor. Susannah Doolittle.

"Fred knocked off an hour ago."

Susannah pushes open the door. "Hey," I say.

She doesn't look at me. "Even so, Miss Precious said
he's not to be staying out all night, that he's—"

"Okay." Fenton looks at me. Laughs. "Fred?"

"You got to remember this is a boy no matter what—"

Fenton hunches his shoulders. Holds out his hands.
Shakes his head at me.

"Come on, Freddy James," Susannah says. "Let's go
have some supper."

I look at Fenton. He shrugs. "I got business out
front." He winks at me. Turns and walks back out into
the hall.

"We'll go over to the diner," Susannah says.

I jump up. I always wanted to eat at the diner.

"Has Miss Precious always been rich?" Just as I'm thinking how stupid I was to down my whole glass of tea
before my meat loaf gets here, the waitress fills up my
glass all the way to the top again.

"Well." Susannah breaks off another little piece of corn
muffin. She doesn't use butter. "Miss Precious's family
had money—her great-grandfather made his at the quarry
—but Miss Precious did them all one better by using her
money to buy up the town." Susannah smiles. Not at me.
To herself. And she eats the corn muffin.

"One day I'm going to make a lot of money," I say.

Susannah nods. The waitress sets down my meat loaf plate. The green beans look a little too hard for my taste, but it still looks good. Lots of gravy. Susannah gets roast chicken. That looks good, too.

"What else are you going to do?" Susannah says. "Make lots of money, and—" She cuts off a slice of chicken. Puts it in her mouth. Raises her eyebrows.

"Well," I say. "Go to war, probably, for a year or so."

Susannah sputters. "War. The war's over, Fred."

"I mean the next one." Far as I've heard, there's always some kind of war starting up.

Susannah blinks. Looks off to the side. Gives herself that little smile again. I'm embarrassed to see how much further along I am with my plate than she is with hers. I slow down. "You had a chance to read that book I gave you? Eleanor . . . your mama said you like to read."

"That *Huckleberry Finn*?"

Susannah smiles. "Yes."

"Well, I started it." I clear my throat. "I don't reckon you got any stories with knights? Or the Trojan War?"

"Trojan War?" She shakes her head. Says something under her breath I don't quite catch.

"Ma'am?"

"Men," Susannah says. "Men and their wars." She sighs. "You like the Trojan War, do you?"

"I like Odysseus," I tell her. "I think he had a right interesting life."

Susannah blinks at me. "I guess he did at that." She

182

pushes away her plate. It's not scraped clean like mine. "I always thought of it as sad, though." She shakes her head. "All that searching. All that trying to get home. All that time lost." Rubs her hands together. Presses them against her chin like she's praying. Looks up at me. "Turned out all right in the end, though, didn't it?" She smiles.

"It sure did."

"How about King Arthur? You like him?"

I've heard about him. "With the round table?"

"Yes," Susannah says. "And there's Sir Walter Scott." She nods. "You'd probably like him."

The waitress sets down two slices of apple pie. I reckon they just come automatic with the dinner. "Ma'am?"

Susannah licks the brown sugar syrup off her fork. "Yes?"

"I sure am sorry. I should have said something before. . . . I'm going to have to pay you for this meal when we get home." I've found that's the best way to save up my money, to just leave it hidden away at home. Otherwise, it's too easy at the end of the day to be hit with the notion of an ice-cream soda. And worse than that, if I come in with money in my pocket, I can't get through the day without wagering it on some silly bet with Paulie or Mitch or somebody. I don't know what it is about Fenton's, but it puts folks in the mind to bet on the sun in the sky and the very air you're breathing. It's hard to keep out of it.

Susannah shakes her head. "This is my treat tonight," she says, "but I won't be coming by tomorrow. I've got students." She points her finger at me. "All the same, you come home. Your mama don't want you staying out all night over at Fenton's."

I don't call her on it, but it hits me that in all her carrying on with Fenton, Susannah hadn't once brought up what my mama wanted. It had all been about what Miss Precious wanted.

I was more comfortable sitting across from Susannah in the diner than I am riding in the front seat of her car. I scrunch up against the door and look out the window. We turn three or four times, but we don't ever lose sight of Miss Precious's big yellow house up on the hill. "How come you don't live up there with Miss Precious?" You'd think she would. It's plenty big enough. And even with all the dust, it's got to be nicer than River Street.

"I'm a grown woman, Fred," Susannah says. "It's right for me to get out and be on my own."

"Oh."

She looks over at me. "I reckon you think moving into one of Miss Precious's own houses, that's not too much on my own."

I shrug. I don't know.

"Maybe it's not." She sighs. "Miss Precious thought it showed a lot of gumption, though."

She eases the car up against the curb and I jump out. "Thank you again, ma'am," I say.

"My pleasure." She sits down on the front steps. "It's too hot to go inside."

I nod and sit down beside her. "Don't let me forget to water Kenneth Lee's garden," I say.

"I took care of that this morning," Susannah says. "And threw Toby his feed." She laughs.

Miss Tinsley across the street lets her cat in and waves at us. "That what you're always going to do?" I ask. "Give those French lessons?"

Susannah smiles, sort of. Only with her mouth. Her eyes look sad and droop down a little lower. "You're wondering what I'm going to do when I grow up?"

"Well, no ma'am, I just—"

She holds up her hand. "I think it's as sweet as can be that little Miss Caroline, those little pilot-struck girls . . . I think it's fine that those tired wives want to spend a little time hearing themselves *parlent Français*, but"— she looks off down to the dark corner where River Street turns onto Main—"I think it's sad and pathetic that they come to a person like me for—"

"No." I don't mean to start her in on anything sad and pathetic.

Susannah shakes her head. "A person like me who learned to speak French from another person like me, who never set foot in France." She looks down. Then looks up smiling. Really smiling. "What I want to do, Fred, is really surprise people one day. To have them look up and say, 'Susannah Doolittle did *what*?' " She laughs. "That's what I want."

We both jump at the clap of thunder. The rain starts

hard and heavy. "Finally," Susannah says. We run inside. "Wait right here," she says.

Every time I study that rug on the wall, I see some new shenanigan or another. One of those dogs is pulling on one of those ladies' skirts. Her mouth is open, like she's yelling, and she's got her horse whip raised up high.

"Here you go." Susannah gives me another book.

"Thank you, ma'am," I say. "Good-night." *Ivanhoe.* I start on up the stairs.

"And Fred?"

I turn around. "Yes ma'am?"

"Just hold on to that *Huckleberry Finn.* You get around to it, you'll find he had himself some adventures, too."

Nineteen

Slow at work today. Slow and sticky hot. The barbecue was exciting, but Fenton hasn't said anything else about doing it every weekend. That whole car business was interesting but they're all gone except for five cars out back. There's a green Chevrolet I figure to talk to Mama about buying when she gets back. Fenton says I can't be driving on the roads in town for a couple of years, but Mama could get her driver's license. That would be something.

With just the niggling everyday matters to take care of around Fenton's, it's easy enough to keep yourself looking busy. Doesn't hurt to have a day like this every once in a while, without something pushing up against you. I almost talk myself into cutting out a little early, but Fenton points out that the woodpile's down to nothing. He's right. I haven't even looked at the woodpile since the barbecue. I give a couple of hours over to building it back up.

I got a dollar and fifty cents in my pocket. I figure I'll just go on over to the diner and try myself one of those pot roast plates. I know how it's done now. Don't worry about finishing off the tea before the food gets to me. The lady keeps it coming. And the pie's not extra if you get the special. The apple was good, but I go for the cherry tonight.

When I get home, I settle in with that *Ivanhoe*. It takes place over in Scotland. Plenty of knights and lords and whatnot, but not as good as Odysseus. I reckon those Greeks can't help but be more interesting, the way they mix it up with the gods and the humans, and those in-between. Anything can happen with those Greeks.

"Fred!" I sit up. Susannah Doolittle. She beats in short raps. She's in the kitchen. "Wake up!"

"I'm in here." I swing up off the couch. I blink. It's pitch-dark out.

She turns on the light in the kitchen. "I just got a call from Minnie Tower," she says. "There's been an accident. A car accident. Get up." She throws a duffle bag at me. "Put your clothes in here."

"Minnie Tower?" Minnie Tower was in a car accident?

"Your mama, Freddy James." Susannah touches my shoulder. "It's your mama." She shakes her head. "That was the only telephone number your grandpa had— Minnie Tower's."

"It's Mama?" I look around the room.

"We got to get down to Charleston," Susannah says. "Meet me out front." She runs back down the stairs.

I take that duffle bag into my room. Rake the stack of clean stuff into Susannah's bag. Put on my shoes. Take all the money out of the cigar box and slide it down deep in my pocket. Go downstairs. Susannah's waiting by the front door with a pillow under her arm. She locks the front door. Takes my bag. Throws it in the foot of the backseat. Slides the pillow in onto the seat. "Climb on in there," she says. "Lie down. Get some sleep."

I know it's not a thing any grown man would do. I know it's what babies do, curling up in the backseat of a car with a pillow. But I do it anyway.

Susannah lets down her window, lights up a cigarette, and pulls away from the curb.

I push up on my elbow. "Susannah," I say. "Is Mama in the hospital?"

"I believe she is."

"And Kenneth Lee?"

"I think so," she says. "Lie down. We got a long road ahead."

I curl up and settle into the pillow. One of the clearest memories I have of Mama is about her wanting to go to the hospital to give birth to Kenneth Lee.

Daddy said it was a crazy idea. Said it would take more than an hour to get there.

"Too far to have a baby," Mama said. "But not too far for drinking and gambling."

"What's wrong with Emmalee all of a sudden?" Daddy wanted to know. Emmalee was the midwife that lived on the Polk place. She was the one that brought me into the world.

"Nowadays," Mama said, "people go to the hospital to have their babies."

Daddy said okay. Said we'd see. If it worked out. But it didn't. Daddy wasn't even home when it was Mama's time. It was me that had to run like lightning over to Emmalee's little house. Beat on her door. Beg her to come. Had to listen to Emmalee's voice go cold and hard as ice.

"She's ready, is she?" Emmalee's face was as still as stone. "I thought she was going into town."

I jumped up and down. "My daddy's gone," I told her. "It's just me and Mama."

That got her going. Emmalee came with me. Moved Mama into the bedroom. Boiled water. Used up all the clean towels. I waited out in the kitchen until Kenneth Lee let out his first irritating little cry. Minnie came over and stayed with us until the next morning when Daddy showed up.

"You wouldn't have made it to the hospital anyway," he said.

"No." Mama was smiling. Holding up my little brother. "He came way too fast." She'd been mad as the dickens up until Kenneth Lee was born. Then she was over it. I'll never forget what she said to me. "Not like you, Freddy James, taking your own sweet time."

She didn't know it, but that made me cry. She didn't

know it, but I was irritated with her and Kenneth Lee for a good long time for all they put me through that day. Truth is, it's not until right now that it hits me. It was all Daddy's fault for not being there. I can't remember why I ever felt any other way.

I jump when the car stops. The sky's an early-morning red. A big blue sign flashes at me. "Oh Susannah!," it says. "Oh Susannah! Diner." Susannah laughs. "Well, that beats all." She turns around and smiles at me. "You hungry?"

I look up at that sign. "Oh Susannah!" It's not until I'm halfway through with my eggs and sausage that I'm for sure that this isn't all just a dream. "What town is this?"

"Pope?" Susannah shrugs. "I'm not sure," she says. "But we've got about a hundred, maybe a hundred and twenty more miles."

"You think they're all right?"

Susannah sighs. "Well, with Minnie I was getting it secondhand, but . . . well, it's bad enough that we need to be there."

"I ought to have been with them." Day before yesterday, it was clear as day to me why I couldn't go. Now I can't recall why that was. Seems like maybe I made a mistake.

Still, if something was really wrong, Susannah would tell me straight out, wouldn't she? And I'm sure that she wouldn't hand me her camera and take the time to have her picture taken with the "Oh Susannah" sign. She stands on the hood of the car—so I can get a good angle—and poses with her arms flung out. Just like that little girl in the picture in her stairway. I take three shots, just to be sure.

What I feel like is climbing in the backseat and curling up with that pillow again, but that wouldn't be right. Susannah's got dark circles under her eyes. The least I can do is sit up front and keep her company.

"How well do you know your grandparents."

"I haven't seen them since I was little, but we've got pictures." I left the pictures behind in the cigar box. I meant to give them to Mama, but I never got around to it. Never thought of how to explain how I came to have them. Didn't want to put myself in a situation where I might have to lie about what else Miss Precious gave me. "We write letters back and forth."

Susannah nods. She drives. I press up against the window. The trees change from pine into palm trees. The dirt on the side of the road turns into sand. The sun gives me a bad headache. After a couple of hours, Susannah pulls into a service station. Looks over her map. Talks to the attendant. "Fifteen more minutes," she says.

Susannah finds the hospital okay, but she drives around it once before she settles on the right place to park. At the first desk, they tell us we want the third floor. We go up some stairs. Stop at another desk. They point us down a green hallway. I ought to step up. Ask some questions myself. But I just follow along behind Susannah. Let her do it all. Worse than Kenneth Lee.

We round a corner to the left. Grandpa Sullivan sits on a chair out in the hall. I know him right away. He stands up. Holds his hat with both hands. Over his heart.

Twenty

My mama's dead. She died a little more than three hours ago. "Hardly a mark on her," Grandpa says. "It was internal bleeding that did it." That's what he tells us, but he has a look like he doesn't believe it himself. "Hardly a mark on her."

Tears roll down Susannah's face. She presses her lips together.

Grandpa looks from me to her and back. Moves his hat from one hand to the other. Sighs. Sets it on his head.

Susannah holds out her hand. Grandpa takes it. "I'm the downstairs neighbor," she says. "Mrs. Tower called me."

Grandpa looks at me. "She said you'd moved off the farm, into town."

I nod. I don't go out of my way to be sociable. I don't have it in me right now. All I can think about is how we wasted time taking that silly "Oh Susannah" picture. When Susannah climbed up on the hood, I giggled about it. My mama's dead. And I'm giggling.

Grandpa looks back at Susannah. "The young fellow—"

I jerk my head up. "Kenneth Lee?"

Grandpa puts his hand on my shoulder. Shakes his head. "Kenneth Lee's fine. He's out at the house." Sighs. "The Fullbright fellow—"

"Where is he?" I just know he's all right. That's the kind of man Custis Fullbright is. To kill my mama and then be all right.

Grandpa nods down the hall. "Banged up quite a bit," he says. "Wasn't his fault, from what they say." Susannah reaches down and holds my hand. "The old fellow in the pickup truck . . . fell asleep, had a heart attack, they don't know what." Grandpa looks at Susannah. "Where's Kenny?"

Susannah hesitates. "We . . . my mama's trying to locate him."

Grandpa's got a look like he's come to a turn in the road, and he doesn't have any idea which way to go. "Now what was she up to with this Fullbright fellow?"

I don't like his tone. Like my mama's done something wrong. I take a step back. My mama's dead.

Susannah puts her hand on my shoulder. Clears her throat. "Custis Fullbright was a friend of the family. He was coming down here on business, so he gave Eleanor and Kenneth Lee a ride." She nods. "I suppose he told you that."

Grandpa looks at me. "You don't know where your daddy is?"

"No sir," I say. "I don't."

His chest just sort of caves in. Looks like he gets a couple of inches shorter all of a sudden. "I reckon we best go on home," Grandpa says.

I look around. "Where's Mama?"

Grandpa's face wrinkles up. Tears roll down his cheek. He shakes his head. "They already took her," he says.

Susannah touches his arm. "Let's take my car," she says. "I'll drive you."

Grandpa sniffs and shakes his head. "You can just follow me out." He holds out his arms to me. Hugs me. I hug him back.

In the car, I scrunch over as close as I can to my door. Susannah waves to Grandpa, up in front of us in a black pickup. What I feel like doing is jumping out of the car and running as fast as I can in the other direction.

"Freddy James?" Susannah lets down her window. Reaches for a cigarette. Hesitates. Slides it back in the pack. "I didn't care much for Custis, either, but Mr. Sullivan's right. It was an accident. Custis can't be blamed for this."

Maybe so, but there wasn't any reason it had to happen. It suddenly hits me that if Big Kenny hadn't up and left us like that, there wouldn't even be a Custis Fullbright. My mouth fills up with that salty taste of tears. My nose stuffs up. I push my face hard against the window. Truth is, I blame Big Kenny.

* * *

We see Kenneth Lee first. He's laying out front in a hammock. His knees are pulled up to his chest. His face is red and splotchy. He gnaws on the fingers sticking out of his plaster cast, but he pulls them out of his mouth right quick when he sees me get out of the car. His face takes on that lost and confused look Grandpa Sullivan's had. "I was asleep, Freddy James," he whispers.

I hug him. I can't remember ever hugging Kenneth Lee before, but surely I did when he was a baby. At least once. I know exactly how he feels. He was asleep. I wasn't even there. Our mama is dead. What kind of story is that?

"It's nice here," he says. "We had fried chicken." Susannah rubs the back of her hand on his cheek. He smiles up at her. "It's like Mama told us."

It is nice. Long lacy curtains blow out from big windows in the front room. "Borrow, Mama?" A lady's loud voice screeches through all that prettiness.

Susannah jumps. A little kid, about four years old or so, runs down the hall toward us. Grandpa hurries through the kitchen door; he was in there getting us iced tea, even though both me and Susannah said we were fine. He points down the hall. "That's your Aunt Sarah." Looks like he forgot all about the iced tea.

Susannah nods. "That must be her baby." I've heard Mama go on and on about her little sister, Sarah, to Susannah. She probably knows more about Aunt Sarah than I ever will.

Grandpa grins. "That's Theodore, all right." He moves past us. Motions us down the hall.

"You and Eleanor were always swapping clothes as—"

"Mama." Aunt Sarah is taller and skinnier, but she has the same hair as Mama. Wavy and thick and piled up in back. Same wide-open eyes. "I'm not saying Eleanor can't wear my white suit, I'm just saying borrow is the wrong word." She throws the white suit on the bed. "Someone can't borrow a suit and then be buried in it." She bounces on the bed. "If you can't get it back, it's not borrowing. That's all I'm saying."

Grandma Sullivan, now she looks just like Mama's photographs, except that her hair's all completely white now. She leans down and fingers the white skirt. She sees me. "Oh my Lord." She claps her hands together. Her cheeks are already streaked from crying, and I can see the tears fill up her eyes again. She holds out her arms. My own eyes fill up. I can't help it. Grandma hugs me. Kisses me. Straightens up. Hugs Susannah. Kisses her on the cheek. Then she steps back. Blinks at Susannah. Like she's made a mistake.

Susannah smiles. "I'm Susannah Doolittle," she says. "The downstairs neighbor. I drove Freddy James—"

Grandma steps right back in. Grabs Susannah's hands. "Oh, you're an angel of mercy, that's what I told James." She looks out in the hall at Grandpa.

Grandpa nods. "It was a mighty nice thing to do, young lady, driving him all this way."

"We all appreciate it," Aunt Sarah says. "You've grown right into a man, Freddy James."

I shrug.

"We're deciding on what . . . on what your mama should wear," Aunt Sarah says. I see now they've unpacked Mama's suitcase. Other than the white suit, it's Mama's dresses spread out on the bed.

"She'd want that dress there, the yellow one with the purple flowers." Aunt Sarah's sitting on it. She looks down. Scoots over.

"Your mama's got some very pretty dresses," Grandma says, "but most of them are . . . informal"— she makes a V with her fingers on her chest—"a little low-cut."

I shake my head. "It's brand-new." I look at Susannah. "She only wore it the one time." I look at Aunt Sarah. "To the barbecue."

"The barbecue?" Grandma looks at Aunt Sarah.

Susannah puts her hand on my shoulder. "Freddy James is right. That's the dress Eleanor would want."

"It's a pretty dress," Grandpa says. "And I think Miss Doolittle would know."

"Well, all right," Grandma says. "Just let me press it." She looks at me. "Do you have a jacket, Freddy James?" Shakes her head at Susannah. "Kenneth Lee didn't bring a jacket."

Kenneth Lee doesn't own a jacket. Neither do I. "No ma'am," I say.

"I told you it didn't matter," Grandpa says.

"They're just boys, Mama," Aunt Sarah says. "And it's going to be hot out at the cemetery."

Susannah takes a step forward. "Miss Sullivan," she says. "Freddy James didn't have but the one white shirt, and he's just completely outgrown it. We were talking on the way over, about how he'd have to try and pick up a new one."

That's an out-and-out lie. I got the one white shirt, it fits well enough, and we never said one word about it.

"Oh my." Grandma pats her hands together.

"It doesn't matter," Grandpa says. "Just anything will do."

Susannah lowers her voice. "It does to him."

They all look at me. I don't like it.

"You have so much . . . so much to think about right now," Susannah says. "Let me run Freddy James into town to pick up a shirt." She sighs. "I want to do something."

"That's so thoughtful," Aunt Sarah says. "But maybe you ought to take a nap after that long drive." She points up. "The extra room's right up—"

"I couldn't sleep right now." Susannah takes my hand. Snaps her fingers and motions for Kenneth Lee to follow her.

"What'd they say about that Fullbright fellow?" Grandma sounds like she's trying to whisper, but she's not doing such a good job of it. "And where's Kenny?"

Susannah pushes out the back door and into her car.

She lets down the window, lights up a cigarette, and says, "I needed to get out of there." We drive off into town.

Susannah never had in mind to just buy me a new white shirt. She drives me and Kenneth Lee into Saultee proper and buys us each a full coat and pants suit. They have white linen, tan, brown, and charcoal gray; Kenneth Lee and me, we both like the brown best. Susannah nods at Kenneth Lee. Scrunches up her nose at me. "I think the gray's better for you," Susannah says. "At your age."

The pants are a little long. "They could be altered by day after tomorrow," the lady says.

Susannah shakes her head. "We'll have to go as is. These are to wear to their mother's funeral."

I sure wish she hadn't said that. "Ooooohhhh." The lady touches her face, my arm, and Kenneth Lee's hair. She clucks. Bites her lip. Shakes her head. It's the last thing I need. The very last thing.

"It was very sudden," Susannah says. "It was a car accident." I will never understand it. Why women feel they got to share their business with strangers.

"Oh my." The lady's mouth flies open. She touches Kenneth Lee's cast. She looks at Susannah. "The Sullivan girl?"

Susannah nods. "Eleanor Johnson. That's her married name."

The lady rubs her cheeks. "That old coot Chester King, we all been saying for years that he ought to be

201

taken off the road and now . . ." She sighs. Holds her hand over her heart. "You boys need ties?"

I look at Susannah.

"Pick out what you want," the lady says. "I'll throw the ties in."

"We certainly do appreciate that, ma'am." The lady wraps up the suits. Whispers a bit to Susannah while she pays.

When we're done, instead of going straight back to Grandpa's, Susannah drives twenty minutes in the other direction. She points up ahead. "Look at that," she says.

I hang out my window. It's the ocean. Mama had shown us pictures, but she said that you had to hear it to really understand what it was. That you had to take off your shoes and run in and out with it. She said it was the ocean that let you know for sure you were connected to the rest of the world.

Susannah parks the car. We get out. Walk down. Sit on the sand for the longest time without saying a word to each other. The water laps up closer and closer to us.

Susannah takes off her shoes and walks down to the water's edge. Looks up at us. Kenneth Lee's right along behind her. I watch them for a few minutes before going down myself. For the better part of an hour we follow each other around on the beach. We keep a distance between us, though. Keep to our own thoughts. I always knew I'd get to the ocean, but I always pictured Mama being there. And Daddy, too.

"Let's go, boys." Susannah waves us over to the car.

Kenneth Lee drags up, climbs into the backseat, and balls up in a corner. His face is still all red and splotchy. We're about halfway back to Grandma and Grandpa Sullivan's when Susannah says, "Kenneth Lee, your mama's going to be so proud of you, standing up tall tomorrow in your brown suit."

"You think so?" Kenneth Lee wiggles up. "You think she'll know?"

"Of course," Susannah says. "And not just tomorrow either. For the rest of your long life into manhood, your mama'll be right there watching over every little thing you do"—she reaches for Kenneth Lee's hand—"so then years and years from now, when you join up with your mama in heaven, you'll be able to talk about all the things you did in your life, just the same . . . just the same as if this tragic accident never happened."

She lies to Kenneth Lee about Mama just as easily as she lied to Grandma about me and my white shirt. I don't see anything wrong with it. Truth is, I think better of her for knowing when a lie's called for.

Twenty-one

Two long rose-colored stained glass windows fill up the funeral home with pink light. The purple-flowered skirt of Mama's dress spreads out wide and full in the coffin. Her hair lays down loose and wavy, down past her shoulders.

The hair was Susannah's idea. There was no question that it would be put up. Mama always wore her hair up, except when she plaited it before going to bed. "Her hair's so beautiful," Susannah said. "Why don't you just leave it down?"

"Just loose?" Grandma Sullivan's face knotted up.

"If she can't let that beautiful hair lay loose in her coffin"—Susannah's voice took that low, sweet, song-like quality—"then where?"

Something about that idea touched Aunt Sarah. Her eyes filled up with new tears. She nodded.

Before the service, Grandma and Aunt Sarah whisper together about whether Kenneth Lee ought to view the body at all. "She's so beautiful," Susannah says. "Like an angel. He ought to see her. He ought to have that to remember."

Grandma Sullivan's mouth pops open. "Oh," she says. New tears ooze out of her eyes.

"Oh my," Aunt Sarah says. "Yes."

The preacher that speaks over Mama really knew her when she was a girl. He remembers Mama singing in the Wednesday night youth choir. "Everybody here must remember little Eleanor Sullivan." He nods right at Grandma and Grandpa. "She rang out loud and clear." I wonder if he's remembering the right Eleanor. My mama used to sing in the kitchen, but she never sang loud. Always very low and always to herself.

We ride to the cemetery in a long black car—what they call the family car—with Grandma and Grandpa, Aunt Sarah and little Theodore, and with Aunt Sarah's husband, Calvin. I'd heard some stories about Calvin, but he's nice enough to me. They say we can squeeze Susannah in, but she says, "Of course not. I'm not family." So she follows on her own in that long line of cars behind us. Mama leads the way, of course, in the hearse.

It's blazing hot out in the cemetery, even if you're family like us and have a place under the tent. A couple of the men take off their jackets. Not me and Kenneth Lee. We wouldn't want to disappoint Mama. Or Susannah.

A girl, not much older than me, sings a sweet song about our heavenly home. Kenneth Lee throws a flower in on top of the casket. He looks at me like he's done something to be proud of. The preacher says some words. Throws a shovelful of dirt in the grave. It's the dirt that does it. It hits us what's happening. Kenneth Lee lets out a scream. They've put our mama in the ground. They're covering her up with dirt. I fall down on my knees and hang over the side of the grave until Susannah reaches and pulls me up.

Kenneth Lee won't get back inside that black family car, so we ride with Susannah in her car. She spends a little time just driving around, so we can get ourselves together. Kenneth Lee gnaws on his fingers. I press my face up against the window. This is the first time, as far back as I can remember, that I don't have some kind of a plan.

Back at Grandpa's, there's all kinds of food. Fried chicken, ham, green beans, potato salad, biscuits, cookies, and cake. I can't eat any of it. Kenneth Lee doesn't have any trouble, though. I sit beside him, over next to the wall, and drink a glass of tea. There's no place to set a plate down. Kenneth Lee has his balanced on his knee. I keep a good eye on it. I'd hate to see that potato salad all over the floor.

Kenneth Lee takes a bite out of a ham biscuit. "Who's taking care of Toby?" he says. "Miss Tinsley?"

I nod. "Toby's fine." I figure that chicken's long gone by now.

"Grandma show you that room?"

"What room?"

"Out back, next to the porch." He stabs up some

green beans. "Grandma's going to clean out her sewing stuff, so it'll be our room."

Our room. I already got a whiff of that idea. Not one person I've talked to has thought anything other than that Kenneth Lee and me were moving in here and staying forever. "Kenneth Lee," I say. "I want you to know this. No matter where you are, no matter where I am, no matter what kind of trouble you come up against, I'll be there for you."

Kenneth Lee slides his plate under this chair. Straightens up and looks at me. "You're not staying?"

"I don't know," I say. "I don't know."

Kenneth Lee nods. Holds up his right hand. Crooks his little finger. I grin. Catch my little finger up into his. "Musketeers," he says.

"Yeah." I squeeze his finger with mine. Give it a good pull. "Musketeers."

Kenneth Lee doesn't let go. "Grandpa said he knows where to get one of those beds that, you know, go one on top of the other."

"Bunk beds?"

Kenneth Lee nods.

"That's what they sleep on in the army." I pull my finger out.

"I'm sleeping up top." Kenneth Lee flails around when he sleeps. He'd fall out, like as not, and break his other arm. "You want to see the room?"

I shake my head. "Not just yet."

That night Susannah offers to switch beds with us. She says the extra bed upstairs is more comfortable, but I like sleeping on the porch. It's cooler. And you're not so closed up out there. If you wanted to, you just get up and walk out the door. Nobody could stop you.

For the longest time Kenneth Lee keeps me awake with his questions. Stupid ones mostly—"You reckon anyone's ever swam clear across the ocean," and the like—but then he asks, "You reckon Daddy'll be down to visit Mama's grave?"

I sigh. Daddy always made a big deal of visiting Aunt Crayton and Uncle Cecil out at the church cemetery on special days like Christmas and Easter. "I think he probably will," I tell him, "but I'm not sure anybody's found him to tell him what's happened."

"Did they look back out at the farm?" Kenneth Lee comes up on his elbow. "He'll need to start the plowing soon, if he's to get in the rye grass on the east field."

I open my mouth. Shut it just as quick. I intend to tell him the whole story about Daddy losing the farm—at least as well as I can—but not right this minute. I give him a little nod. "That's right." I roll over. After a few minutes Kenneth Lee's breathing slows down. He slings out his right arm. Kicks me. He's asleep.

Now I'm hungry, so I slip inside and rummage around until I find some of those ham biscuits. I sit outside on the steps and eat them. Picture Daddy throwing himself on Mama's grave. Holding onto a big beautiful stone with her name on it. Crying and crying. I reckon he ought to be.

Even after I climb back in bed, I stay awake for the longest time. Thinking over all Kenneth Lee's questions. Even the stupid ones.

I wake up to the sweet smell of Grandma cooking pancakes and sausage. The smell's about all I can handle, though. My stomach can't take more than one of each. It's a good thing Kenneth Lee keeps Grandma happy, eating one pancake after another, just as fast as she can keep them coming.

I'd made sure last night that Susannah understood I was going back to Elderton, but when Grandma sees my bag packed and ready to go, too, she's surprised. She looks over at Grandpa.

"Where do you think you're going, son?" Grandpa says.

"We've got that apartment I need to clear out," I tell him. "I'll call you on the telephone when we get there." I do mean to move on out of Elderton—last night it came to me there's nothing holding me there anymore—but I never say I'm coming back to Saultee. I know that's what Grandpa and Grandma hear—they hug me and smile—but it's not what I say. I need some time to get my thoughts together. To make a plan.

It's a relief to be back in Susannah's car. Moving. "Where do you think we might find somebody to make a gravestone?" I ask.

Susannah looks at me. "A marker?"

"I want something more than a marker. I want something that sticks up out of the ground." I reach down into my pocket. "I've got seventy-two dollars to spend." I wonder what happened to that twenty dollars I gave Mama. I'd planned to pay Custis Fullbright a visit and ask him about it outright, but Grandpa said he'd already gotten out of the hospital. He was gone.

Her eyes open wide. "Seventy-two dollars." She taps the wheel with her fingers. "Did you mention this to your grandpa?"

"No ma'am." Didn't see as I needed to. It's my money and my mama.

She sighs. "You know, your mama might rest easier knowing you had that money for your . . . your future."

I shake my head. "I want to get Mama a stone." That's the only sure thing I worked out last night.

Susannah gets directions from an old fellow walking by. Drives down a side road to this neat little brick house. Gravestones stick out all over his yard. Like flowers.

"How much you looking to spend?" he asks.

I keep that to myself. "How much would that one run me?" I point to a real big one, done up in a sort of pinkish marble. And it's curved and fancy on top, not just plain flat.

"That one's fifty dollars, son," he says.

"Mama would like that color." I look up at Susannah. "And I want a saying on it. Not just Mama's name."

"Saying's going to run you extra," the man says.

I think. I think about Mama. I think about Minnie Tower; sugar water; clean, folded clothes; and double-chocolate devil cake. I think about her hand over my forehead, checking for fever. About field peas and cornbread and the ocean.

Susannah's full of poetry. "Do not go gentle?" Something about death is slumber.

A little drizzle starts up. I think about Mama's brand-new yellow dress, buried down in the dirt. And how now it'll get wet, too.

"A Bible verse," the man says. "That's your best bet."

I try to stop it. It's no time to be crying, when you've got seventy-two dollars in your pocket to deal with. I walk away from the both of them. I want to walk away from everybody.

Susannah follows me. Puts her hand on my shoulder.

I don't look at her. I've cried plenty of times, just like anyone else, but I've always been able to stop. To just sniff the tears back and get rid of them. But I can't. I can't hold back. "If it was Daddy—"

"Miss Precious, she's trying to get hold of your daddy."

I shake my head. All Daddy's sayings rattle around in my head. All about being a man and the principle of the things and setting the tone. "If it was Daddy—"

Susannah gives me a handkerchief. I blow my nose. That helps.

"If it was Big Kenny," I say, "it would be easy to come up with something." I look up at Susannah. She looks so sad, I feel bad for acting like such a baby. She looks so sad, it puts me in mind of that picture of Bucky Kent in her secret stairway. All those pictures. Puts me in mind of Mama slouched and sad in that chair. Because she didn't have her yellow dress yet. I blink. Blow my nose again. "Mama said—"

"Yes?" Susannah probably wants to get this over with.

I see the man standing over with his stones, looking at us.

"Mama said if you loved someone, and they loved you back"—I squeeze my eyes shut. How was it she put it?—"you can't ever be rid of them." I nod. That's it. "Not even if you want to."

Susannah smiles. "That sounds like Eleanor, all right." Nods. "Let's do something with that."

We come up with "Because she loved us, and we loved her back, she will always be with us." The man says he'll be done in ten days and will put it at the head of Mama's grave for me. I pay him sixty dollars. I've got twelve dollars to get on with the rest of my life.

Twenty-two

"You want to stop to eat at Oh Susannah's?"

"No," I say. "I'm not hungry." I hope Susannah's pictures turn out okay, but I don't want to see them. And I don't want to ever see that place again. I don't want to think about how I was giggling around while my mama lay dead.

"Okay." Susannah taps her fingers on the wheel. "Your grandma and grandpa, they seem like nice people. I think you'll be happy there."

I lay my head back against the seat. "Yes ma'am." I look out the window. Those palm trees sure are strange. All bunched up on top like that. I feel light-headed and confused. Try to figure whether I'm going to or going away from someplace. I just don't know.

"We will have to stop to eat at some point," Susannah says. "I can't let you starve. You're in my charge."

I sit up straight. "Can we go through Columbia?"

"I imagine so," she says. "Get that map out of the glove compartment."

She pulls to the side of the road and stops. Unfolds the map over the steering wheel. Traces out a route with a finger. "Shouldn't be a problem," she says. "Might even be better." She folds the map back, exactly the way it was. "What's in Columbia?"

"A barbecue place," I say. "This mustard sauce barbecue Fenton told me about."

She shrugs. "We'll ask around. We'll see."

We stop at a service station for gas, and the attendant knows right what we mean. "Morris's," he says. And he knows right how to get there.

"Must be a popular place," Susannah says. "That's a good sign." Barbecue's not her favorite food. I overheard her say that when she told Mama she wouldn't be coming over to Fenton's Fourth of July party. "But then," she said, "Fenton Calhoun's not my favorite person." But she doesn't mention that today, and I'm not passing up this opportunity just to be nice.

She's not that thrilled once we get there. "Okay," she says, "we've got a choice." She sighs. "Do we eat from trays in our car, or do we go inside and sit on those wooden benches?"

"Inside." I hold open the door for her and read the sign on the other side of the door: "Help Wanted/ Counter Boy."

"Fred?" Susannah points up at the board. "What looks good."

I close the door and look up and down the list. "The Big Plate," I say. I watch the boy behind the counter take our order from Susannah. He rings it up on the cash register and gives us our iced teas and a number. Not five minutes have passed before the waitress calls out 24 and serves us our food. It's a pretty good system.

Susannah cuts her sandwich into four tiny little parts. "It's not bad," she says.

The Big Plate comes with French fries and coleslaw and bread on the side. It's great. And I swear, if I took some of it back to Dorothea, she'd say so, too.

Susannah tries to make a little conversation, but I don't feel up to talking. She stands up. Looks around. "I hope this place has a ladies' room," she says.

I take the chance to finish up without her trying to talk to me. There's a counter with pitchers filled up with iced tea. A sign says "Free Refills. Help Yourself." That's a good idea. That's convenience. I look around at all the people. Nothing confusing about Morris's. It's an eating place.

I get up. I reckon I ought to hit the men's room myself before we get on the road. When I come out, I peek in the kitchen door. A waitress rushes through. "Everything all right?" she says.

I nod. "Great." I lower my voice. "Who would I talk to about getting a job here?"

She points out a fat man behind the cash register. "Morris," she says.

Susannah comes up behind me. "There you are." She takes my arm. "We better get on the road."

I roll up into my side of the car. Close my eyes. I

wonder what Mama would have done, if we'd had us a place like Morris's. Wait tables or work back in the kitchen. Or stay up behind the register. I reckon me and Mama and Kenneth Lee would have to do a little bit of everything.

Susannah lets down her window. Lights up a cigarette. Pulls out and waits at the road for a line of cars to pass. "You do know," she says, "that Miss Precious will do whatever she can to help you out."

"Yes ma'am." I'm paid up through next week, but after that there's no need for the apartment. That was for Mama and Kenneth Lee. And even though I appreciate what Miss Precious has done for me so far, I think I've had about enough of her help. I don't want to end up like my daddy, taking so much that I end up losing what I've already got.

I sit up straight. "Susannah?"

"Yes?"

"About how long you think it took us to drive from Saultee to Columbia."

"Oh," she says, "about an hour and a half."

I nod and settle back into my corner. Truth is, there's no need for me to stay on in Elderton. I'm getting a little tired of all the goings-on at Fenton's, and Fenton can always find himself another boy. Working in Columbia, I'd be close enough to check in on Kenneth Lee from time to time. And if I could get on at Morris's, I could learn a little more about his system.

When I open my own place, I ought to call it Eleanor's,

after Mama, but the truth is, while Eleanor's a nice enough name for a lady, it doesn't set the right tone for a business. Truth is, I'd pick a place called Big Kenny's over an Eleanor's any day of the week. I couldn't do that, though. It just wouldn't be right, with all that's happened.

Now Mama's middle name is Ruth. Ruth's Restaurant. That's got a better sound to it.

"Freddy James?"

I look up at Susannah.

"I just think you ought to remember that even Odysseus had Athena to help him along on his journey now and again."

"Yes ma'am," I say. "I reckon so." Trouble was, that Athena was always done up in some crazy disguise or another, and Odysseus never really knew who to trust. I press up against my door, close my eyes, and don't wake up until we pull onto River Street and stop.

Susannah unlocks the door, and I slip past her. She follows me halfway up the stairs, but I close the door on her. I just don't feel sociable. That hot, musty, closed-up smell smacks me in the face. I open up the windows, stretch out on the floor, and let the little bit of evening breeze blow over me. Kenneth Lee's book he borrowed from Susannah is on the floor, right where he left it. *The Three Musketeers*. A piece of brown paper sticks out near the end; I reckon he didn't quite get through it.

I sit up and flip through the book, trying to locate

that "All for one" business, but I can't. I hear Susannah's back door slam. I get up and look outside. I ought to say something, no matter how much I feel like just being by myself. I ought to at least say thank you for driving me all the way across the state and back.

Kenneth Lee's garden droops down and lays on the steps. You can tell it didn't rain a drop while we were gone. I fill up a bucket at the sink, take it down, and water around the roots of his zucchini and tomatoes. Smile over at Susannah sitting on her steps.

She smiles back. "I can get you some boxes for packing," she says. "Those bags won't travel too well on the bus." She shrugs. "Or train. Whatever."

"Yes ma'am." It'll have to be the bus. I hear it's cheaper. The tomato plant perks right up. I run up and get another bucket of water for the beans.

"You planning on fixing a big supper?"

I nod. "Yes ma'am." I reckon I have to. There's a pot load of beans and about twelve ripe tomatoes. And there's always way too many zucchinis. I could probably sell a little up and down the street. "You want some."

She laughs. I figure she's laughing at the idea of eating my cooking, but I look up and see it doesn't have anything to do with me. She's laughing at Toby, who comes strutting, just as pretty as you please, from out behind the pecan trees. I can't believe that bird's still here.

"You going to just give it back to Dorothea?" Susannah asks.

I shake my head. "Kenneth Lee seems to want it down there."

Susannah frowns. "Well, I don't think it's a good idea to just be packing up a live chicken and sending it down as baggage." She gives me a hard look. "They might take it, but the heat will probably kill it."

She's right. I toss out an overripe tomato. Toby pecks around at it. I find it mighty strange that Toby didn't just fly away. The Greeks put a lot of importance on birds showing up—took them as a sign—but I don't know if they'd make much of a chicken.

I sit down on the bottom step and pick a caterpillar off the zucchini vine. "Well, then," I say, "I reckon I'll just have to hand carry it down to Kenneth Lee myself." I could do that. And, truth is, I don't see any way around it.